UNNATURAL SELECTION

A Fantasy Adventure Novel

WRITTEN

By

Ed Wode

Published by:
Horned Toad Productions, Inc
Long Beach, Ca 90810-2730
U.S.A.
All rights reserved under International and Pan-American convention
Contact:
edwode@gmail.com

Distributed by:
www.lulu.com and HTP, Inc
ISBN: 978-0-6151-4292-0
copyright © 2007
by Ed Wode

UNNATURAL SELECTION

Chapter 1.

Evolutionary Headquarters

From the penthouse window of a skyscraper metronome a man peers through binoculars at the tiny figure of a woman far below who is seen to be approaching. This most unusual building is a 1000-foot tall working metronome with a recording studio penthouse on the top floor. There is the very loud tock-tock sound characteristic of a metronome that can be heard for miles around.

As the woman gets closer she is seen to be carrying what appears to be a cheap suitcase covered with place pennants. She looks urgently around and up from time to time. When there begins to be the sound of bloodhounds in the distance, her urgent look turns to a look of extreme horror. Suddenly the sky appears to be full of voluptuous red lips dripping long red wet tongues that are licking and laughing, barking & snapping at her. The woman screams and runs until she comes to the front door of the giant metronome. The sound of the ticking has now become deafening. There is a sign over the door that says, "Metronome Records, a division of Evolution, Inc. Uninvited groupies beware". JUSTINA-JANE WANE ignores the sign and enters the giant timing mechanism in extreme panic.

JUSTINA walks around the cavernous windowless space shouting "hello", but is only answered by the echo of her steps and own voice. When she gets to the center of the room, she looks up just in time to see a giant black spider descending on a thread. She is paralyzed with fear as the giant spider stops in close proximity to her. A deep resonant voice speaks to her and tries to calm her fears. The soothing voice from above speaks to her.

"Don't be afraid my dear. BLACKIE is my living SPIDERVATOR. She is very gentle ...with mad suicide bombers. Groupies must beware. She can snack a groupie before you can say floor 100, my cozy penthouse-recording studio. However, you have nothing to fear, my dear. Mount her and stroke her head. She will bring you directly to GOD. Me that is." (A big masculine basso laugh)

JUSTINA does as she is told and has an uneventful, if hairy ride to the 100th floor penthouse of rock music star, GOD ZIMMER, president of Evolution, Inc. This corporation owns the country of Evolutionland and GOD ZIMMER is both president of the corporation and the country. As chairman of the board, he is authorized by the corporate by-laws to use the title God. JUSTINA dismounts from SPIDERVADER directly into the luxurious penthouse pad of GOD ZIMMER who is sitting in a Jacuzzi reading a girlie magazine.

GOD ZIMMER mistaking Justina for her twin sister JANE speaks to her like a long lost friend.

"JANE WANE! My favorite secret agent terrorist bomber. Welcome to the headquarters of Metronome Records, a division of the country of Evolution, Inc. I am GOD ZIMMER, lead singer of the Rollin' Stogies, God of the board of Directors of Metronome Records, President of the country of Evolution, Inc. and head of the Celestial Intelligence Agency, your humble boss, agent Wane."

JUSTINA manages to calm her fears.

"What happened to America?"

GOD ZIMMER with obvious matter of fact unconcern answers glibly.

"It went belly up and downsized into the state of N. Carolina, smoking mandatory from age 10 to 100. The rest of the states were sold off to various fortune 500 companies like this one."

JUSTINA is visibly unhappy to hear this.

"Ugh... Poor America. At least those scalp-taking gamblers who claim to be Indians don't own it. When they captured me, I was almost scalped. Then I had to smoke a whopper of a stogie they called a peace pipe before they would let me go. That Chief, ugh..."

GOD ZIMMER with thoughtful bemusement commiserates with JUSTINA.

"You mean CHIEF HORNY TOAD WHISPERER? That perverted Indian is no respecter of tourist attractions. When he captured the Alcatraz Free University Theme Park from us, the dumb shit turned it into a casino and let blackjack dealers go topless. Our former tenant Disney is really pissed. They don't do nudity ...yet. The high rollers flocking there now might make them change their minds though. This Indian Pearl Harbor means war with us. That's why you're here. But how did you manage to keep your hair?"

JUSTINA blushing with embarrassment tells her tail.

"He scalped the warden and tortured me in every kinky way. I managed to keep my hair by a clever ruse. I smoked stogie peace pipe with the whole tribe. But, I am no longer a virgin, MR. GOD sir! (Said like a tearful military grunt) Am I still your favorite secret agent sir?"

ZIMMER becoming lasciviously excited answers her with elevated interest.

"You did the whole tribe? Good work. I wrote the manual on the peace pipe smoking trick. You are promoted to agent 0069, my favorite kind. And here's a signed copy of the manual. Don't worry, my dear, you're safe now. And call me Maestro. I think God's a little intimidating don't you?"

JUSTINA is most agreeable.

"A mite. Just a mite. But God is what most people like to call you."

ZIMMER with an air of utter contempt gives his opinion of the human race.

"Most people are retarded assholes. That's why I avoid them as much as possible. I especially hate prayers. So much noise. And they think I'm here to be their personal valet. I could stop a Tsunami with my little finger if I wanted too, but I can't be bothered."

JUSTINA is genuinely surprised at the difference between this God and the one she has been taught to believe in. This guy doesn't seem like he would help a blind man cross a freeway in the dark.

"You could stop one? I thought your indifference was to give us a fling at free will. But why did you take mine? Those bloodhounds of yours wrangled me right up to your doorstep. I've never been so stressed in my life."

ZIMMER somewhat apologetically states his case.

"With your reputation as a compulsive-obsessive bomber you can't expect me to let you wander around unescorted. You might inadvertently bomb some of my fans. Come; join me for a relaxing Jacuzzi. I want a blow by blow description of how those kinky Indians tortured you."

JUSTINA goes to the CD player and puts on some strip tease music. She does a very sexy striptease that leaves God Zimmer panting and leering, long tongue dripping, much like his bloodhounds. She then climbs naked into the Jacuzzi with him.

ZIMMER is ecstatic.

"Well-done 0069. That beats genuflection by a light year."

JUSTINA turns on the sexual innuendoes to please his ego.

"It must be gratifying to have millions of people stroking... your ego and bowing to you every day."

ZIMMER with a certain amount of false pride explains where he is coming from.

"I used to get a rush out of it, but organized religion has been taken over by a bunch of charlatans who are more interested in market share than morality. When I look into people's hearts where they try to hide their deepest darkest secrets, I see that instead of wanting to be something useful like Angels, they want to be rich and famous loafers like me. Great TV show, but I hate imitators."

JUSTINA coyly strokes his ego.

"You can't blame them can you? You made them in your image. And you've promised to reward the biggest fanatics with seventy virgins. I'd like that."

ZIMMER slyly reneges on his word.

"If I had seventy virgins to give away to every dumb yahoo so called martyr, you think I'd be sitting in this Jacuzzi alone reading girlie zines? And besides it was only three. Humans have a greedy talent for exaggeration."

JUSTINA dummies up.

"I don't know where people get such fantastic ideas."

ZIMMER affects mock anger.

"From self appointed saviors. Where else? But a woman of your superior intelligence repeating such rumors... You surprise me."

JUSTINA affects contrition.

"Sorry, I banged my head on a hypothetical banana peel."

ZIMMER gets a big laugh out of this. He is now on the make big time and goes into a macho braggadocio mode.

"My apologies too, my dear. I didn't mean to intimidate you. I don't want to come off as a bully. That's what those lousy atheists think of me, thanks to so called organized religion. Boy are they in for a surprise on judgment day. Have you ever seen how fast a 400 lb. atheist glutton genuflects when he sees me sitting on my corporate throne, in all my glory, getting a pedicure from my favorite mass murderer?"

JUSTINA enthusiastically shines him on.

"Which one?"

ZIMMER with an amused air tells his secret.

"The one with the funny little Charlie Chaplin mustache. He gives great foot fetish while we listen to that Wagner noise he likes so much. What a megalomaniac. He thinks he's the greatest toe sucker in the universe."

JUSTINA in mock shock appeals to Zimmer's conscience. As she will soon discover, he doesn't have one.

"Surely you haven't forgiven that fiend his transgressions?"

ZIMMER exudes affected integrity.

"You expect me to make an exception in his case?"

JUSTINA affects righteous indignation.

"Don't you think that's carrying forgiveness a tad too far?"

ZIMMER is even more righteously indignant.

"My laws may have a few flaws my dear 0069, but inconsistency isn't one of them."

JUSTINA becomes submissively contrite.

"Anyway, you're the boss. What's my new assignment?"

ZIMMER gets serious and more down to business.

"Did you bring a sample?"

JUSTINA replies stoutly, "You betcha".

ZIMMER is apprehensive as hell, but pretends to be enthusiastic. "Let me see. I've never seen one before it was used."

JUSTINA gets her suitcase that contains a nuclear bomb and opens it for GOD ZIMMER, very near Zimmer.

ZIMMER is fidgety and very nervous.

"Wow, that's a beauty, but what's that funny writing?"

JUSTINA tells him, "Russian."

ZIMMER pontificates sententiously.

"What a perfect corporate state the Soviet Union had when it called itself Communism. A shame they went belly up. That's what happens to corporations when they don't focus on the core product. Soon as they closed the gulags things started to fall apart. (Stroking the nuke) A few of these babies Fed Exed to D.C. would have had a profound effect on whether the 21st century was to be the American century or the Russian century. That could have been the perfect first strike and they didn't even have to waste money on rocket fuel. Now it looks like it's going to be the Chinese century, because America is pissing its resources away trying to run the world pro bono. And I refuse to learn that absurd ping-pong language. I just hope those Chinamen never get religion."

As Zimmer is going on, he is lusting over Justina who is naked as a jaybird demoing the nuke very close to him.

JUSTINA aware of Zimmer's discomfort both sexual and nuclear teases him with sardonic relish.

"Did you just want to get a rush ogling this baby or you want a real live demo? Just push this button right here... I mean the nuke button. Don't worry, Gods are immune to nukes."

ZIMMER is really terrified, as he answers her.

"No demo, it might frighten... BLACKIE. How many have we got?"

JUSTINA boldly brags.

"100" Maestro sir."

ZIMMER answers happily.

"Perfect. The board of directors has decided its time to make another example like Lot's wife."

JUSTINA affects disagreement.

"Another pillar of salt? But why? There's no shortage of salt."

ZIMMER is slightly exasperated.

"There's going to be a shortage of gospel singers if we don't stop those Indians from converting everybody into gamblers. We're about music."

JUSTINA bravely stands her ground.

"But why get your fig leaf in a bundle? If they didn't bribe the politicians somebody else would".

ZIMMER patiently explains his dilemma.

"The board hates competition dummy. This company is as crazy as a Hollywood film studio. Our whole team could get booted to that wormhole where people are Chinese-speaking termites. You can't even drink a cup of coffee without swallowing a couple dozen. We have to constantly remind ourselves that we are about Evolution. That means we want lots of babies. Males and females coupling by the rules of natural selection. Look around you at the people you know. What do you see?"

JUSTINA looking around with an air of total amazement says, "Why... of course! Unnatural selection. How stupid of me not to have noticed! God! Opps, forgive me Maestro.

Took your name in vain again. I'll donate my bra to the curse fund. You are right about needed reforms Maestro sir. But how're people going to shag if we blow them up?"

ZIMMER becoming in character as the arrogant boss he is gives her a little demonstration of his Godly powers along with her marching orders.

"Listen dummy, you're not paid to think. You are ordered to set those things off in 100 cities that have Indian gambling. We've got to get those unnatural selectors back in line 0069. I want every one of those oohs and aahs paid for from now on. I want babies! I want pain! The board wants lots of babies or they want my scalp. Make music, don't gamble! Now, get out of here unless you and MAGDALINA would like to... Never mind. (As he says this, he SHAPESHIFTS into a beautiful nude woman and there is a big insouciant female laugh.) Go, Go! Business before pleasure."

JUSTINA leaves the metronome. A taxi pulls up and she jumps in, leaving her suitcase on the sidewalk. The driver gets out and loads it up. JUSTINA in a hurry tells the driver to take her to the airport.

"Go, take me to the Evolutionland Airport fast. I've got to make a flight to Seattle.

TAXI DRIVER familiarly answers, "Right away MissWane".

JUSTINA, "How do you know my name?"

"Bosses orders Miss Wane."

They take off in a cloud of dust to a nearby airport. Justine grabs a plane to Seattle to see her psychiatrist boyfriend Dr. Michelangelo Marconi who has an office in Seattle and San Francisco.

Chapter 2.

The Maoist Transvestite

JUSTINA is lounging back on a psychiatrist's couch talking calmly to DR. ANGELO MARCONI, who has very large red lips. DR. ANGELO MARCONI wears what he characterizes as a Red Chinese type of uniform that could be easily misinterpreted correctly as a red dress. DR. MARCONI is JUSTINA'S, kinky androgynous psychiatrist boyfriend and fellow terrorist.

JUSTINA describes Zimmer.

"You should have seen this stud who claimed to be God. He even changed into a woman and made a pass at me. Can you believe it? GOD, a shape shifter?"

ANGELO impatient with lust goes for the gusto.

"It was just another of your hallucinations probably. Nothing contagious. Just to be on the safe side though, I better check you for breast cancer."

ANGELO puts his hands in her shirt and fondles JUSTINA'S breasts as JUSTINA squirms with pleasure.

JUSTINA enjoying the exam to the point of becoming hysterical says excitedly,

"I can't take anymore of these hallucinations Dr. Marconi. Please try to help me. Oh, oh, aah... That's some help, but don't stop. I need a real pope size exorcism."

ANGELO is sweating with hypocritical lust. He takes a contemptuous tack in order to play hard to get.

"Everything seems to be normal except the size. I don't usually examine such small size gropers. Why don't you come back after you've gotten some hi tech feely friendly implants?"

JUSTINA responds negatively.

"I need help now, DR. MARCONI. Please. You're a psychiatrist aren't you?"

DR. MARCONI is friendly now.

"Yes, but I really wanted to be a gynecologist."

JUSTINA screams bloody murder...

DR. MARCONI worried about the neighbors, answers contritely. "O.K, O.K. I'll help. But tell me, who's the son-of-a-bitch that referred you to me?"

JUSTINA lies imaginatively.

"I was sitting on the crapper at the airport reading graffiti on the wall and it recommended you as a psychiatrist who helped runaways. I'm not exactly a runaway, unless you consider escapees from the nut house to be runaways. But I am running away from some megalomaniac terrorist who claims to be God and wants me to nuke 100 cities."

ANGELO is impressed.

"You've got to be a freakin psychoid of some kind. Why would God want to blow up 100 cities? I may have to give you a more thorough examination."

JUSTINA pulls out all the stops.

"If I give you the world's greatest blowjob, will you still think I'm crazy?"

ANGELO takes advantage of JUSTINA'S kindness.

"If you want to know the truth, I'd think you were a raving lunatic, because there's no condom in the world that can hold back my lethal ejaculation. But don't let that stop you. Insanity, like virtue, has its own reward."

JUSTINA takes up the challenge.

"You are pushing me too far DR. MARCONI. You see this remote. You're not going to grope me or any other sucker again if you don't cure me of being a hit woman for God."

ANGELO is intimidated slightly.

"Calm down my dear. I know what it is to suffer. Believe me, more than once I have wanted to scream and rant and rave and there has been no one to comfort me. I sometimes have to cross dress to calm down."

JUSTINA pretends to be concerned.

"Oh, you poor man. You may be a bit kinky, but you are kind. I'm sorry I had to threaten you to get you out of the closet."

ANGELO has his confidence back and resumes his psychiatric persona.

"Let me make a small correction in your analysis, my dear. I am kind of kinky, but very unkind. Now, let's get your story straight. Did you escape from a garden-variety loony bin or were you maxed for being a big bad criminally insane pain-inflicting psycho of the world-class kind?"

JUSTINA, "The latter!"

ANGELO, "What exactly was your specialty?"

JUSTINA, "I was lethally obscene. I blew up random assholes."

DR. MARCONI is very curious about assholes.

"Tell me why. Assholes interest me".

JUSTINA explains how she came to become a terrorist.

"Well, after I sneaked in to the movies and saw Lolita, I developed a compulsion for blowing up gropie old men. Then, I started blowing up bland condoms they gave away in junior high. After that, I got a job picking up dog poop."

DR. MARCONI is curious, "So?"

JUSTINA finishes the wax job.

"Have you ever tried walking around all day picking up used condoms with a pooper-scooper? It's exhausting. That's why I became a terrorist"

ANGELO confesses a heart felt bond to JUSTINA.

"My dear, you can feel right at home with me. I too am a terrorist. And this is where I make my bombs. If you walk really good dog, I may be able to get you a fellowship grant to study with me."

JUSTINA is not impressed.

"You, a person sworn to heal people, want to blow them up? Did you take the hypocritic oath by mistake?"

ANGELO gets nasty. In spite of his lust for JUSTINA, he is no sycophant.

"Hypocrisy is not nearly as dumb or crude as your specialty of blowing up bland random assholes. I have developed my own original healing hypocrisy. And it has a humane side. Like, I am planning to blow up the Golden Gate Bridge during rush hour."

JUSTINA gets excited.

"During rush hour! But my dear! Is that really humane? Just think how many poor suffering souls that jump from the bridge every day you are keeping from such beautiful suicides?"

ANGELO with great pride waxes egotistical.

"Yes, I know; but think how many more people I can save from suffering in traffic everyday?

JUSTINA is crestfallen at her perceived incompetent lack of anticipation.

"I never thought of it that way."

ANGELO is now on top of his game.

"That's the problem with undisciplined loonified female terrorists. You are too carefree. I plan to change all that."

JUSTINA really blows her top.

"Are you sure you're playing with a matched set of brain cells?"

ANGELO becomes a menacing bully.

"Have you perchance noticed my huge red lips? Didn't you say something about having red lips in the belfry?"

JUSTINA is not intimidated.

"Are you the monster who has been stalking me? You are lewd looking. And why do you wear that ugly red dress? The whole outfit looks like it came from a Salvation Army fire sale. And your make up! Ugh..."

ANGELO answers her with great pride.

"Oh? You don't approve? This is the latest Maoist capitalist haunt couture uniform. And I'm all Victoria's Secrets underneath."

JUSTINA jokes, "Are you sure you don't have a red-hot Italian wiener fetish?"

ANGELO sneers back intellectually.

"I wear this uniform as a symbol of my solidarity with the Red Lip Stalin Path of Peru. The Inca people trying to bring back communism after 500 years of white man's capitalist tyranny."

JUSTINA tops him sneer for sneer.

"Isn't that kind of a retarded bunch? Communism went out with Freon around the turn of the millennium."

ANGELO stumbles under the onslaught of JUSTINA'S logic.

"Most of the world's population lives under Freonism... I mean, Maoist capitalism."

"Maoism in name only", she insouciantly rhapsodizes.

ANGELO'S retort effectively defeats her insouciant narcissism.

"And the world is free of Freon in name only. The hole in the Ozone gets bigger every year and so does China under Communist Capitalism."

"Maybe Maoism and capitalism were made for each other."

"Is that your healing hypocrisy"? she asks.

"The last empress of China was a horny toad. She was so fat she could hardly drop a load."

JUSTINA is revolted by his insensitivity.

" You are unkind. Listen, DR. MARCONI..."

"Why don't you call me ANGELO?"

JUSTINA comes down to earth with an expensive thud.

"Listen Angelo baby, this is costing me a fortune. Can we talk about me for a while?"

"Drivel up! It's your dime, JUSTINA baby."

"My real name is JANE WANE. After the death in combat of my identical twin sister JUSTINA, I assumed her identity. My escape began on the day of the red eclipse. We were in the exercise area of the free university, as the public knew the concentration camp, and suddenly we heard Indian war drums…"

Chapter 3.

The Indian Invasion of Alcatrazland

As JUSTINA tells her story of the prison to Angelo, island buildings begin to take on a 3D holographic realness. ANGELO listens in wide-eyed wonder as he sees this virtual reality take shape. Prisoners are surrounded by walls and guard towers. A courtyard appears and in it a large group of women are doing aerobic dancing when the sound system cuts out and there is the sound of Indian war drums. The prisoners start dancing like Indians. The sky goes from blue to blood red and there is the war whoop of Indians as they land in an armada of boats. The identical twin Wane sisters stop dancing and talk.

JUSTINA WANE comments on the drums to her twin sister JANE.

"That's the signal for the forces of freedom to attack."

The GUARD excitedly speaks to the prisoners.

"Attention prisoners! Stop dancing to those subversive drums. We don't recognize that noise as music." He snaps a

whip at them. "It's only those virtual Indians showing off."
As he says this, an arrow goes through his hat. "Damn those careless game designers. This is a real arrow."

The Indians swarm over the walls and quickly capture the guards and prisoners. The female prisoners have taken the whip from their aerobic guard and turned it on him. The Indians scalp him and set the women free, with strings.

The INDIAN CHIEF holds up a scalp.

"Sorry ladies. It's gross, I know, but it's in my genes."

JANE WANE speaks the mind of the rest.

"Indians on the warpath in the 21st century? Is this a joke?"

The CHIEF assures them it is not.

"You are now trespassing on the sacred burial ground of the Alcatraz Indians. The Shining Path Stalin Inca Corporation, subsidiary of the country of Red Lips Stalin, Inc., takes possession of Alcatrazland in the name of the Inca. The Buffalo have returned. We will soon open here on this site our one-thousandth casino. Prisoners are free to go if you smoke Rollin' Stogie peace pipe. We also offer retraining of prisoners as blackjack dealers, Indian dancers or human sacrifices. Long live the Inca."

"Can I be a topless blackjack dealer", JUSTINA implores the CHIEF?

"That's an immoral suggestion, but maybe it'll bring in more high rollers than Remington paintings. I'll see what I can do MISS."

"How can my sister JANE and I get off this rock chief?"

The CHIEF offers a dishonorable ransom.

"If you give good peace pipe, we will call a helitaxi for you. Come to my tent."

JANE and JUSTINA are taken to a tent where many braves are sitting in a circle waiting to smoke a peace pipe. Back on the mainland, ANGELO is following the situation. He is watching the invasion action on a laptop from a camera on a satellite via a program ala Goggle Earth that looks down on the prison yard. He is trying to locate JANE WANE. He is employed to find her.

"Looks like the WANE sisters have been smoking peace pipe. That chief loves to make peace almost more than taking scalp. (His cell phone rings and he answers) 'Freedom taxi service here! Yes Chief. We'll send a copter right away.' (To a pilot standing by) O.K., go! Take JANE straight to GOD ZIMMER. Leave her kooky sister someplace else. Like in the ocean from way up. Be careful or she'll blow you up. And give this Mickymoto pearl necklace to that Indian chief. Those Indians love beads."

The PILOT is incredulous.

"But, is that beads scam going to work in the 21st century?"

"He's a cross dresser, dummy. Now go."

The pilot takes off. JANE & JUSTINA'S ordeal from smoking a great deal of the tribe's peace pipe is almost over. They are a little wobbly from the trial by stogie, but are waiting quietly for a helicopter at an Alcatrazland helipad. The Chief is waiting with them for his payoff. The CHIEF is smoking a Havana cigar.

The CHIEF graciously offers a cigar to the ladies.

"Want a real Cuban cigar? It's a good change of pace from that Rollin Stogie."

JANE still frazzled from being gang banged takes a hit.

"Can I have one toke? I'm still wasted from your peace pipe. For an old fart, you sure can swing Chief. I just want to go home."

The CHIEF reassures her.

"A helicopter is on the way."

JUSTINA is ecstatic.

"Free at last! CHIEF, I owe you one and you'll get it in the mail. Hey! There's the helicopter on the way."

JANE is feeling uneasy.

"It's almost too good to be true. I smell a skunk somewhere."

The CHIEF reassures her.

"It's my cologne, Royal Skunk for men."

JUSTINA starts jumping for joy.

"Here it comes."

As JANE & JUSTINA wait, a scalped guard regains consciousness. He is furious at having been scalped and fires at JANE as she is boarding the helicopter. She is hit and falls inside on the floor mortally wounded. The helicopter takes off. JUSTINA is crying hysterically.

The pilot shouts, "Hang on. We'll be at a hospital in a few minutes."

JUSTINA now hysterical shouts, "Hurry!"

JANE is calm and resigned.

"Don't worry about me. I've had it."

JUSTINA is sobbing inconsolably.

"Don't talk like that."

JANE tries to reason with JUSTINA.

"Promise me you won't forget the things I've taught you. You must assume my identity and continue my work. It is a great honor to be a terrorist for God."

JUSTINA is now softly sobbing and accepts her sister's ministrations.

"Dear JANE, don't die. You know I'm a menace to the natural order of things. I'm incompetent. I'm loony. There is no way I can ever fill your shoes. You must hang on or your work will die with you. I refuse to be a human sacrifice."

"You'll be O.K. DR. MARCONI will save you."

"That phony. He's a monster. His lies and deceit are what got us sent to Alcatrazland."

JANE presses her case.

"You must trust him my dear. DR. MICHANGELO MARCONI holds the key to evolution. He will not let you be a human sacrifice."

JUSTINA disagrees.

"He's a pervert."

JANE offers her personal philosophy.

"Life is a battleground, my dear. A burning lake of liquid fire inhabited by greedy glutinous monsters that must sooner or later devour us all. Pride is to fight bravely and die laughing."

"I hate living and am afraid to die. Oh JANE dear, what's the use of fighting?"

"To overcome stupidity. To shed one tear of truth among an ocean of lies makes it all worth it, JUSTINA dear."

"I'll try. I promise you I'll try, my love, but please don't die."

JANE is fading fast.

"Good-bye honey. Let your feelings be your guide to the eternal kingdom of you. I die."

The PILOT is in tears.

"Is she???"

JUSTINA is sobbing lightly again.

"Yes she is."

The PILOT now assumes control of the situation. He has heard JANE'S admonishments to her sister JUSTINA and decides to honor them. This means that he must ignore his instructions from ANGELO and let JUSTINA assume her sister's name and duties.

"You had better assume your sister's identity. Fuck ups are not allowed to live in Evolutionland. GOD has an important assignment for JANE, but he will probably throw you to his hellhounds if he finds out you are not JANE."

"Who is this GOD? And what makes you think I'm a fuck up?"

The PILOT becomes worried at her defensiveness.

"The one living GOD. GOD ZIMMER. I am taking you there."

"Yes, take me to him Mr. brazen PILOT. Gods are not in any playbook I go by. I want to see him or her as the case may be."

Just then there is a flash of light from the ground. A missile hits the tail rotor and it breaks off. The copter spins crazily to the ground. It crashes, but the occupants survive the crash. JUSTINA is dazed, but miraculously unhurt.

The PILOT tells JUSTINA the bad news.

"We've been hit and we're going to crash."

The copter crashes and the pilot is mortally injured. His brave dying words are...

"We have crashed in the holocaust ruins. Look for the JUDGE. He will give you a road map. You will receive a valuable suitcase at the snake tollbooth entrance to the Tock-Tock highway. Take the suitcase and go to GOD ZIMMER. To find Him, listen for the sound of a giant metronome 1000 feet high. There you will find GOD ZIMMER in his penthouse on the 100th floor of Metronome Records. Compliment his singing and all will go well. Here is some money for the toll." He hands her a jar of desiccated small animals. "Beware of the snake's breath." (He dies)

Chapter 4.

The Judge-Prosecutor-Defense Attorney Combo

JUSTINA in a panic jumps out of the copter and begins to run. All around her are the ruins of what used to be San Francisco. As she runs, suddenly there are phantasmagoric figures all around her. The place is an apocalyptic holocaust ruin occupied by rag-tag remnants of humanity. They close in on her menacingly. A bloody dazed JUDGE is just in time to save her. The JUDGE is holding court in a sedan chair carried by slaves. He is passing sentence on passersby who are unlucky enough to cross his path. They are hauled away by bailiffs, put in stocks and whipped.

"I find you guilty and the evidence is all around you," he says to no one in particular. He repeats this endlessly until he is accosted by JUSTINA.

JUSTINA recognizes the judge.

"You are the self-satisfied asshole who sent my sister to Alcatrazland. I blew you into fish flakes and I am as happy as a hungry goldfish."

The JUDGE threatens her.

"GOD will blend your soul in an atom masher and reincarnate you as a quarky string martini."

JUSTINA taking the physics challenge rebuts the JUDGE'S string theory handily.

"GOD is an obsolete quantum computer program. Whoever's calling the shots now has about as much compassion for the human race as a cross-eyed piranha has for a lamb chop."

"God has no need of compassion. He is a judge, my dear."

JUSTINA goes new age ballistic.

"And I am evolution's first female with buckie balls and a crystal dick."

Holocaust victims begin to chant while closing in on JUSTINA for the kill.

"Death to sluts! Death to sluts!"

JUSTINA finds this very funny.

"I just wanted to cure my oversexed nightmares with some nymphoid daymares."

The angry victims give her no quarter.

"Give her a makeover with a two-inch wiener."

JUSTINA makes a joke at everyone's expense.

"A hangman judge and a hangman jury. Here's a partnership that's sold out to the hemp lobby."

VICTIMS take hold of JUSTINA and chant.

"Burn the witch at the stake."

JUSTINA stands up to the threats.

"Who you calling a witch, bitch? I'm a card carrying witch bitch buster."

The victims take hold of a kicking screaming JUSTINA. The JUDGE intervenes.

"Wait, this one should have a trial. She has the mutilated soul of a martyr. Let us pre-empt her by giving her a fair trial. Now, for my opening statement."

JUSTINE cries foul.

"Wait! Are you both judge and prosecutor?"

The JUDGE demurs sarcastically.

"An excellent example of the trend toward making democracy safe from hypocrisy, don't you think?"

JUSTINA replies sarcastically.

"If you polish my butt with rouge, I'll throw myself on your mercy and plead for more."

The JUDGE is really pissed off.

"You won't get off that easy. I have a job to justify and by Buddha's pierced belly button, I'm not going to lose it because of Kamikaze defendants. I appoint myself as your defense counsel as well and I plead not guilty on your behalf. Now let's have the first lying witness for the prosecution and you better remember your lines."

JUSTINA sarcastically demurs.

"Judge, prosecutor and defense attorney? This must be a privatized court."

A VICTIM comes forward to testify.

"You blew up our plane. There were 6000 half lab rat, half human victims."

JUSTINA pleads not guilty.

"Oh dear GOD! I made a terrible mistake. This action was a protest against the use of animals for medical experiments. I didn't know those rat-looking humans had rat genes. I should be ground up and put into hot dogs sold at ball games. I admit guilt for not checking the cargo manifest better, but I'm innocent of intentionally taking pure Arian human life."

The JUDGE rules as JUDGE-PROSECUTOR-DEFENSE-ATTORNEY. "As prosecutor, I love hotdogs. As defense, so do I as long as they don't have hair… As judge, I overrule bald dogs! I only eat real shaggy hot dog, but we'll take this matter under consideration until after lunch. Next witness."

A FOOTBALL PLAYER who is on crutches and bandaged from head to toe takes the witness box.

"Oh! She adds insult to injury. Next she'll want to make popcorn out of cockroaches."

The JUDGE is getting hungrier by the minute.

"That's one of my favorites too. What's your complaint, if you have one young man? And it better not be about any of my favorite snacks."

"She made a booby trap out of a football and it blew my record setting 100 yard field goal kicking leg off."

JUSTINA shows no remorse.

"Sports are the opiate of the people."

The JUDGE rules, as wisely as Solomon.

"This witness is disqualified, because he is a drug dealer. Next witness."

HARVEY HOFFMAN wearing dark glasses and walking with a cane like a blind man hobbles up to the witness box and is sworn in. He is a world-renowned schlock movie director. He testifies angrily, "She threw acid in my eyes. I can barely see my masterpieces."

Remorseless as a prosecutor, JUSTINA accuses, "You complain of your vision when you never had any?"

"I gave people what they wanted to see. Am I not kind?"

JUSTINA rags on him fiercely.

"Listen snow brain. Is it kind to corrupt the innocent and give birth to national insanity?"

HARVEY sneers back.

"It doesn't take any Socrates to know she's the abominable snapping pussy."

The JUDGE is beginning to be a convert to JUSTINA'S cause.

"You know, as JUDGE, I think I'm beginning to understand your case my dear. HARVEY, I cite you with contempt of humanity, the worst crime there is. Feed him to the piranhas, alive." HARVEY is dragged off to the fish tank screaming. "As defense counsel, I make a motion to dismiss the charges on the grounds that love of animals is a crime of passion and crimes of passion are not recognized as crimes in the 21st century. As prosecutor, I object to this motion on the grounds that bombing a plane is an intellectual protest in no way passionate or sexual. As judge, I rule the motion for dismissal is granted on the grounds that the defendant committed this heinous act to keep all animal species from being polluted with human genes. Especially my favorite, the endangered hissing cockroach or is it the rare anal anteater... never mind. Case dismissed. Bailiffs, clear the courtroom. Come my dear. We can have a snapping tête-à-tête in my stretch limo while we figure out how to get you safely away from here. You've got to go someplace, anyplace or you'll be lynched on sight here at holocaust denier central."

"I'm looking for the road to revolutionary headquarters. I hear you can help me find it."

"You bet I can, my dear."

The JUDGE gives orders to whip the protesters. The protesters are beaten back as the JUDGE and JUSTINA take off. JUSTINA gives the JUDGE a real lip-lock kiss as soon as they are alone in the limo.

"Oh JUDGE baby, you're so much fun."

The JUDGE gives a quick summery of his career. "That makes 9074 cases in a row I've won as a defense attorney."

"But you the prosecutor lost."

The JUDGE is as cold as frozen pussy.

"Yeah, but he gets paid anyway."

This segues from JUSTINA lying provocatively back in the stretch limo waiting for the judge to make a move to JUSTINA lying back on a psychiatrist's couch just as provocatively talking to ANGELO in his Seattle hide out safe office.

Chapter 5.

The Revolutionary Psychiatrist.

JUSTINA, yawning with lust, challenges ANGELO to behave like a gentleman.

"Thank you for listening for a change."

"After what you just told me, I think I need a drink. Can I offer you some brandy?"

"Just a sip."

ANGELO pours a little in a glass, hands it to JUSTINA, and then pours himself one. ANGELO toasts her nutty story sarcastically.

"Salute to that tale JANE or JUSTINA. Are you positive, which one you are?" He laughs derisively.

"What's so damn funny, ANGELO honey?"

"You expect me to believe all that psycho rubbish about GOD and cross dressing Indians? Especially the part about the nukes." He laughs again.

"I warned you, you Maoist pervert."

JUSTINA pushes a button on her remote control. The ground shakes and there is a mighty roar. She has detonated a small N-bomb that takes out the Space Needle in Seattle and a few blocks around it. They are ensconced at a safe distance in a nearby safe house. There is a horrendous noise that breaks some windows in the house. ANGELO is shocked at the tremors.

"Wow! What the hell was that?"

"I took out the Seattle Space Needle and a few blocks around it. Mostly Bill Gates' hideaways for female computer hackers I expect."

"Yes, that was the porno web site builder district too, but what does Gates need with hackers?"

"Geek female hackers are the biggest sluts. You know a male that doesn't like a slut?"

"You have something against sluts JUSTINA? Some of the best people are sluts."

JUSTINA feels highly insulted.

"No stupid. I hate monopolists and sluts monopolize the easiest men. They are worse than sexual tourists."

"What have you got against sexual tourists?"

"You weren't a wannabe nympho slave prisoner working as an aerobic dancer in a tourist trap like Alcatrazland or you would know."

"You're a nympho aerobic slut? Now things are starting to make sense."

JUSTINA is contemptuously angry at his error.

"I said nympho, not slut. You believe me now or should I blow the next one up your nice tight ass?"

"Sure I believe you. You have to take out Seattle's main landmark to prove your point? There are plenty of skid rows around you could have demonstrated on."

"You just don't get the point do you?"

ANGELO is starting to sweat marbles, "Well..."

"O.K. buster. You asked for it."

ANGELO starts to plead.

"JUSTINA, JANE baby. Dear 0069, I want to hear the rest of your story. Really!"

There's a great rush of wind and ANGELO rushes to cover a window that has been broken by the blast. JUSTINA quite nonchalantly tells Angelo that it is radioactive fallout.

"Don't worry. It's just radioactive wind. Eat a lot of iodized salt and you'll be fine."

ANGELO rushes for the kitchen cabinet, pours a bunch of salt into a glass of water, and drinks it with a brandy chaser. He almost barfs, but manages to keep it down. He then offers some to JUSTINA, but she declines.

"No thanks. I take these iodine pills I picked up at Hiroshima. They're a lot easier to swallow. Can you believe, they're made in North Korea and cost as much as Viagra?"

ANGELO is furious and looks like he is going to attack JUSTINA, but calms down when JUSTINA points the remote at him.

"That's a good boy. No more male bully tactics or you'll be sucking up angel dust. And I don't mean the kind they make to give to poor helpless animals. Now, can we continue?"

ANGELO picks up a pipe and lights it. He then collapses into a chair glaring at JUSTINA.

JUSTINA settles down to continue her story.

"I met some nice people on the way here who tried to hip me up on the way things have been evolving since I was on the rock. They were real GOD ZIMMER fearing evolutionaries. They said you embodied the most advanced stage of dialectical perversity known in the universe."

"Naturally of course. I'm a Maoist capitalist."

JUSTINA curious asks, "How does one, eh... become officially recognized as a Maoist capitalist?"

"It only took the change of two or three words in a new Chinese constitution."

JUSTINA is much surprised.

"You're kidding. Two or three words made people Commie Capitalists?"

ANGELO lets his intellectual hubris hang out.

"Yes, the old Chinese communist constitution was tyrannizing the government. It made the government responsible for finding over a billion people jobs, but the new 1982 Chinese constitution gives every one the freedom to find their own job. How's that for freeing the slaves without firing a shot?"

JUSTINA is much impressed.

"Great suffering succotash. That's what I call progressive hypocrisy on a grand scale with a capital H."

"But enough of this political trivia. What did you do with the other 99 bombs my dear one?"

"They're in 99 lockers in 99 cities, ready to be set off by my satellite controlled GPS remote."

"So we've evolved from the sword of Damocles to the remote of terrorists like you. Where do we go from here?"

"What's that you're smoking there ANGI baby?"

"Jimmy's old hat. You want to try some?"

"Who the hell is Jimmy?"

"He's a friend of mine who wears clothes made out of marijuana. You want to try some?"

ANGELO hands the pipe to JUSTINA and she takes it. After having a few deep inhales she continues her story.

Chapter 6.

The Beautiful Young Man

JUSTINA smoking with ANGELO segues into JUSTINA smoking a pipe in a forest clearing sitting on a fallen redwood stump deep in thought about how this beautiful redwood forest has somehow survived man's ubiquitous depredations. As she is doing so, a beautiful butterfly lights on her arm. It is a very small humanoid female who is able to speak to her.

A tiny BUTTERFLY WOMAN speaks to JUSTINA.

"What seems to be troubling you my dear?"

JUSTINA maintains her cool.

"I'm thinking about all these trees that lived thousands of years immune to fire, insects, disease or other ravages. Only man has been able to destroy them. What is man? Is he a blight on life?"

The small butterfly surprises JUSTINA by changing into a full size woman.

"Oh! Where did you learn that trick?"

The BUTTERFLY replies modestly.

"It's no trick. It's our nature to change when we're ready. I too am human. Just a tad more creative than most people."

"How about you? Do you destroy every living thing in your path?"

"I like to suck the honey out of the honeysuckle. I like to beat the pollen with my wings."

"You sound like a real screamin' meanie."

The BUTTERFLY takes a liking to JUSTINA.

"How would you like to borrow my spare set of wings? I can show you around a bit. Maybe you need a wee bit of a peak at the big picture."

"You... You sure it would be all right?"

"Sure! Nobody tells me what I can and can't do with my spare wings."

JUSTINA puts on the butterfly wings and she and the butterfly woman take off to see the world. Flying is a little strange to JUSTINA at first, especially butterfly flight that is a little less than straight as an arrow. They constantly land and take off on waiting blossoms where they gorge themselves on delectable honey. In no time they are covered with all manner of pollen. At each flower they visit, they shake off the pollen to the rhapsodic oohs and ahs of happy pollinated flowers. Finally, they land in a tree with thousands of other butterflies.

JUSTINA has had enough of this weird kind of flight.

"This is it for me. I can't take crowds. I'm out of here. Thanks for the tour. It's a beautiful world when you look at it through a butterfly's eyes."

"Humans are destroying everything. I hope you can help stop the blight, as you call it."

"Don't worry. I've been assigned to nuke the blight. But how do I get out of this jungle?"

"Why don't you ask that young man sitting by the pool over there?"

JUSTINA flies over and lights on the arm of a beautiful young man dressed in golden raiment.

"Hey buster. How do I get to Revolutionary Headquarters?"

The godlike young man, who is the reincarnation of Buddha before he gained weight, spies the butterfly on his arm talking to him and waxes poetic.

BUDDHA composes a love poem to JUSTINA:

"Lovely naiad resting gently on my golden bough. I praise thee, so like a water lily in thy grace, so like a butterfly in thy face. There you are open like a new plum blossom, my summer hope of fulfillment. I hold thy nectar sweet in my heart, the world of passion's truth, encompassing in thy immortal form, all that is dear to man or God.

JUSTINA falls instantly in love.

"Hey, I'm human just like you. Damn, I want to be big again."

As she says this, she regains her full size by falling off his arm into the pond. She still wears the same flimsy chemise she had on as the butterfly. Wet as the shift now is, it leaves little to the imagination. BUDDHA helps her out of the pool.

"For a naiad you don't swim very well, but your growth rate is amazing."

JUSTINA now provocatively ready for action quips back lustfully.

"Not half as amazing as that poem you just recited. It's got me all turned on. My nectar is positively percolating."

"What's your name naiad that you dare voice such profane thoughts to Siddartha?"

"Let's get things on the table Sid. You just wrote me a love poem. You want to get it on or not golden boy? It's been, notwithstanding the dunk in the pool, a bit of a drought for me."

BUDDHA laughs heartily.

"I'm sorry..."

"What's so damn funny? Am I so repulsive?"

"You don't understand. I'm a God."

JUSTINA'S frustration boils over.

"Boy-o-boy, this is my week for meeting the nutcakes. Does Godhood keep you from doing the horizontal rumba? Never mind. My hormones are in cardiac arrest anyway."

"I did not know water nymphs had desires. Desires are very bad for you."

JUSTINA has had it with this guy's jiving her.

"How do you think we reproduce? We lay eggs like turtles. Somebody has to have a yen to fertilize those eggs."

BUDDHA doesn't see, but answers her politely.

"I see."

"Maybe you better watch more nature movies on TV. They show you all the gory details. It's better than being a farmer's daughter"

BUDDHA is confused.

"I see, but what's TV? I don't understand."

"Are you sure you're O.K., Sid? You could get satellite T.V. right here. A couple of solar panels hooked up to car batteries for energy storage, and you'd be able to watch old movies 24/7."

"But I have my dragonflies, my bees, my water lilies and thee."

"I give up. Can you help me Sid? I'm looking for the Tock-Tock road and I'm lost."

"Yes, that's easy. Blow this conch shell horn and when you get an answer, go in that direction."

"Sid my friend, I can see there's substance behind all

that glitter even if its gold plate."

JUSTINA takes the conch shell and blows it several times. Finally there is an answer and she goes off in that direction.

"Thanks Sid. If you're ever in my neighborhood stop by and we'll watch some re-runs."

BUDDAH doesn't have a clue.

"Re-runs?"

Chapter 7.

The Tock-Tock Road

JUSTINA is still in the beautiful redwood forest. She does not get very far down a redwood path before a very large snake confronts her. He has a very unpleasant human face. His name is MEAN SNAKE.

The intimidating SNAKE speaks to JUSTINA.

"I am MEAN SNAKE, the toll collector for the Tock-Tock Freeway. Do you have the toll?"

JUSTINA tries being an intimidating wisegal.

"If it's a freeway it should be free."

MEAN SNAKE is less than polite.

"It's named after a favorite song of the boss. You still have to pay."

JUSTINA takes out her purse.

"How much?"

MEAN SNAKE demands a lot.

"A nice fat skunk and a Komodo Dragon for desert."

"My, you do eat well. The best I can do is two dead horny toads, a large leaping lizard and a no longer hissing cockroach. You got any change?"

MEAN SNAKE starts to get mean.

"No change girlie. You must have the exact amount; same as on a bus or I keep the change. Any way, that's not even enough for desert."

JUSTINA starts to get mean.

"You better get the hell out of my way or you're going to look like a blue plate special sushi kabob at Benihana's of Tokyo."

"I am going to eat you alive sweet meat."

JUSTINA assumes a Kung Fu stance.

"I've heard that threat before."

The snake attacks JUSTINA and she Kung Fu kicks the critter almost senseless.

"I knew that Kung Fu training would come in handy sooner or later."

It is quite a battle for a while until JUSTINA tries to go around the snake and is tripped up. The end of the giant snake's tail grasps her and it winds around her until she is head to head with the snakes mouth.

The SNAKE is right in JUSTINA'S face.

"Any last words before I swallow you?"

"Yes, use some Breathalyzer."

"It must have been that skunk I ate for breakfast."

"Here's a couple of Breathalyzer toads and keep the lizard for a tip."

"Can I have the hissing cockroach for desert obnoxious lady?"

"Just when I was getting hungry, but I'll make the sacrifice. You can have the whole jar."

"I'll let you go then."

Just then a Fed Ex truck drives up and delivers a suitcase to JUSTINA.

The FED EX DRIVER yells, "Package for JANE WANE."

"That would be me", she lies.

"Sign here."

JUSTINA signs for the tattered suitcase covered with place pennants.

"Thank you MISS WANE."

Chapter 8.

The Challenge to a Game.

JUSTINA has fallen asleep while she is telling her story and ANGELO has wrapped rope around her tying her to the couch. He is sitting next to her eating an apple. When she wakes, she thinks he is the snake in the Garden of Eden.

JUSTINA screams bloody murder.

"Get that apple away you slimy, slithering, slippery snake in the grass." She manages to head butt Angelo. "Try to tempt me you red fruit. Take that, you Maoist woman molester."

ANGELO is knocked to the floor writhing in pain. JUSTINA gets loose and begins to hurl things at him. He staggers toward safety with blood running from his nose and takes refuge behind a large stuffed chair.

"MISS WANE! MISS WANE! Please come to your senses. You are raving like a madwoman."

JUSTINA goes into a blind rage.

"You tried to attack me... and wearing

a dress." She picks up a large object and starts to throw it.

"Stop JANE or you will be the death of both of us. There is a bomb hidden in that vase."

JUSTINA snaps out of her trancelike state.

"MICHOANGELO! It's you. I thought you were a snake in a dress."

"Sorry, just a Maoist capitalist in the dress uniform of the people."

JUSTINA has a complete change of heart.

"You know ANGELO, in spite of my hatred of male chauvinist pigs, I find you enormously attractive. You look so sexy in your dress uniform. And your large red lips make you look like the Angelica Joli of revolutionaries."

"Large lips go hand in hand with an expanded mind, my dear"

"Yours must be enormous."

ANGELO is expansively boastful.

"Yes, I admit I have an abnormally expanded I.Q."

As JUSTINA has become outrageously provocative, ANGELO has an enormous erection. She is strutting her lewd side cock teasing him unmercifully.

"I wouldn't mind smoking up some of that I.Q. ANGELO baby."

ANGELO becomes introspectively analytic.

"I just wish I could figure out some way of getting rid of that subversive alter ego of yours JUSTINA. Your pseudo sister JANE is obscenely provocative. To have such an original idea of morality is lewd and unpardonable. The whole world could be infected with this psychic disorder. If evolution has taught us nothing else, it has taught us that ideas are more infectious than the most virulent disease."

"Spare me the psychic ball job ANGELO."

ANGELO is not to be out jived by anyone.

"I have finally reached a diagnosis of your disease my dear. You are suffering from galloping nymphomoralmania. The prognosis of this disease is bad. You'll probably be napalmed at the stake or crucified on a hairy rabbit."

"Isn't there any cure?"

ANGELO has sprung the trap. He has his quarry where he wants her.

"Only mental terrorism has been able to cure this heinous disease. Fortunately for you, I am a protégé of Chairman Mao."

"And I suppose your success rate testimonials call this a better mental diet than a lobotomy."

ANGELO spins enough hubris to soak up an ocean of overweening pride.

"I cured the whole country of China. Think of it. One quarter of the people of the world having rid themselves of nymphomoralmania at one stroke of the pen. You must let me undertake to cure you. I won't rest until those obscene red lips breathe their last foul breath."

"I feel safe now. Do you love me ANGI?"

ANGELO attempts to maintain dominance, "I cannot sublimate your sublimations and keep my license. Besides, love is a game played between two false prophets. We are for real."

"Let's play a game for profit."

ANGELO is intrigued. "I don't usually play games. What kind of game you have in mind?"

"It's called Amnesia."

"Amnesia?"

"Yes. Amnesia! The idea is to make me forget who I am. If you succeed, you can shag me. If you fail, I can shag you. Want to play?"

"The winner gets to screw the loser? This sounds like a game for oxymorons, but I accept the challenge anyway. Let's start. Are you JUSTINA or JANE?" (He laughs)

"You will find out when you kill the false me. And stop laughing. This is a serious game. If you can't take it seriously, I'm going to nuke San Francisco to steam."

"For the love of God Zimmer, don't preempt me. I take games very seriously. Next week I'm going to blow the Golden Gate Bridge."

"You've only got one hour."

ANGELO panics. "One hour! This'll take a mortar shot to the center span." He opens the back of a Charlie Chaplin lamp that exposes an electronic heart. Isn't this a beautiful low yield nuke mortar shell? Just enough megatons to do that center span."

"No stupid. You misunderstood. You've got one hour to win the game."

"What have you done for evolution, JOHN WANE?"

"I wrote the macho manual of violent sex, but I am no JOHN. I want many children."

"You are guilty of petty bourgeoisie revisionism comrade. Chairman Mao said, 'Having children is a tactical error.' I love you Jane."

"You're a man with chameleon principles ANGELO. You don't love JANE or me. All you want is my lipstick on your expedient stogie."

"Blow up your mind and get a life JANE. Your sister JUSTINA is not the real you. She salivates for me. Do you?"

"You're a loser fool ANGELO and losers don't evoke salivation. You're not woman enough to win this game even if you do wear a dress."

"You wear pants. Why can't I wear a dress if it cures evolutionary neurosis."

"Your evolution is the dictatorship of bad taste. I hate imitators. Let me go before I vomit."

ANGELO becomes seriously threatening when his good taste is challenged.

"Not before I lobotomize your hot panting cock teasing terminal tits. I'm going to tune you in to the great psychic ball job. The eternal orgasm of your affirmative desires. There is no confusion except your sexual delusion."

"And piss tastes better than puke. So what? I'm out of here Angelo. Find some other bimbat to douche with your unmanly threats."

ANGELO grabs her and forces her down on the couch. JUSTINA pretends to be helpless, as she waits her chance to clobber him.

"I will never let you go. It is the manifest destiny of the Maoist capitalists to penetrate you. You'll be gobbled up by the ever watchful, leering, laughing and liquidating red lips. There is no way to get out of here until I've ejaculated on your counter cultural climax."

JUSTINA knees him in the crotch and escapes his clutch.

"Why can't you treat me like Sleeping Beauty ANGELO and penetrate me when I'm having a wet dream?"

"What you really need is a flu shot. Put your big mouth butt in my hands."

JUSTINA bends over provocatively and hikes her dress up above her waste, sticking out her butt.

ANGELO produces a large syringe, as if by a magic trick.

"I faint at the sight of large needles. If you're a man, shove it in when I'm not looking and make me squeal like a pig."

JUSTINA is still holding her remote and pushes a button as ANGELO pushes the needle into her. The ground shakes and there is a rumble in the distance.

"What was that?"

"A dam on the Columbia river just got nuked. This remote has a hair trigger and that needle tickled me until I had a nuclear orgasm. I think I can hear the Salmon cheering. No more locks."

"No more lox and bagels. God Zimmer will be furious JANE."

ANGELO is standing there in shock with a large needle in his hand. JUSTINA takes off out the door. ANGELO'S shiny red motor scooter is sitting in the driveway with the keys in the ignition. JUSTINA jumps on the unguarded scooter and rides away

Chapter 9.
JUSTINA Meets a Hip Rabbit.

JUSTINA is riding down the highway on ANGELO'S shiny red motor scooter when a very large RABBIT comes hopping across the road almost colliding with her. He is wearing a tuxedo coat with tails, a top hat, spats and not much more. He sort of hops along and pauses when he sees JUSTINA who has braked to keep from hitting him.

"Miss, may I inquire as to where I can seek refuge from the hounds on my trail?"

There is the sound of hounds. They are the same hounds that were tracking JUSTINA to Revolutionary Headquarters and are not far in back of the RABBIT.

"Hop on. I know how to get away from those hellhounds."

The hounds burst forth from the forest just as JUSTINA and the rabbit take off.

"Just in time or I would have been GOD ZIMMER'S rabbit stew dinner tonight."

"I'm trying to find PROFESSOR WONDERFUL. Do you happen to know where he lives?"

"Yes, but it's not in a better part of town. It's near the slaughterhouse. I'll take you there, but why don't we stop by my place first and freshen up. I've gotta great pad with a bar and other amenities. And rabbits are immune to aids."

"Oh, oh... I was wondering what was sticking me in the rear end. And it tickles."

"You sound like you're prejudiced against big hairy wazoos?"

"No, but I'll have to take a rain check. I'm on a mission for GOD ZIMMER."

"You work for that genocidal maniac?"

"He thinks so, but I'm really in business for myself."

"Get off at this exit. My house is just nearby. God booby trapped too, in case you turn me in."

They leave the main highway and turn off on a dirt road. They soon come to a mailbox that says, "NOAH'S ARK JIMMY". JIMMY jumps off the motorscooter.

"I live in this three-story condo right here in the ground. You're welcome anytime."

"Your name's JIMMY? You the one who wears the smokeable clothes?"

The same. Here, you can have my coat and hat for saving my life. Best smoke you'll ever have."

JUSTINA who is still almost naked in the pretty transparent dress she has been wearing since the escape is much taken with JIMMY'S coat and hat, but she is reluctant to accept a gift from someone who lives in a hole in the ground.

"But I can't..."

"Don't worry about it. I've got a hundred more growing down below."

Out of desperation, JUSTINA accepts

"I don't know how I ever can repay you."

JIMMY comes on very strong.

"Just slide down my rabbit hole pole sometime when you're not so busy. Be sure to keep your shaggen wagon snapping and ready for action. My waterbed is right at the bottom of the hole. Wear some of Victoria's Secret carrot flavored edible undies please."

"I'm pretty busy this week and I have to cleanse a Texas safari next week. But when I can find time I'll put on my best kinky bunny carrot flavored edible playboy bunny outfit and come over. But hey, I thought you were going to take me to PROFESSOR WONDERFUL'S house?"

"It's easy from here. Just go down that dirt road until you get to a brook of pure running pig's blood. When you get there, follow it till you come to a slaughterhouse. Ask the guard at the gate where you can find PROFESSOR WONDERFUL."

"Bye-bye JIMMY. I'll be in touch soon."

When JIMMY opens the door to the condo hutch, a multitude of little rabbits swarm him crying, "Daddy, you're home."

JUSTINA feels like she's been turned into a home wrecker bimbo by this Lothario rabbit.

"Next time I see you buddy, you're going to be horny rabbit stew."

Chapter 10.

Professor Wonderful's Gadgets

JUSTINA pulls up to a guardhouse on her motor scooter. There is a river of blood gushing out of the slaughterhouse past the guard shack. There are horrible screams coming out of the slaughterhouse.

JUSTINA is taken aback by the human sounding screams.

"Those screams sound almost human. What kind of animals do you slaughter at this packinghouse?"

The GUARD tells JUSTINA the horrible truth as nonchalantly as if he were talking about manufacturing pecan pies.

"Pigs mostly. Although people who can't get life insurance because they have bad genes are also some-times added to the sausage to give it flavor."

"I have heard people and pigs taste a lot alike."

"It depends on the kind of feedlot hormones they have been fed. Some of them taste like skunk. Especially liberal politicians."

"I have been told that Professor Wonderful, head scientist of Evolution, Inc., has his laboratory here."

"That is top-secret information. You a spy for some Indian tabloid?"

"I am GOD'S personal representative. Let me go in."

"I don't care if you're the Pope in drag; you haft to arrive here in a cattle car to get in without a password."

JUSTINA points her remote at the guard and SPIDERVATOR appears. JUSTINA laughs.

"Whoops wrong password button. I'll never get the hang of this new remote."

The spider almost eats the guard before he panics.

"Go, go, go, and Try the National Front for Cockroach Control on the fourth floor. And get this GOD damned SPIDER off me."

JUSTINA manages to turn off the living-hologram just in time.

"There, I hope you're happy. I saved your life. Have a nice day."

JUSTINA enters the slaughterhouse elevator and pushes the button for floor four. When the door opens, technicians in space looking suits take hold of her and put her in a disinfectant chamber. She is stripped naked and given a sterilization shower. Finally, she is given a sexy skintight sterile outfit and brought before a precocious looking juvenile who arrives and takes charge of the situation. He is PROFESSOR WONDERFUL, the fifteen-year-old wunderkind head of R & D for Evolution, Inc.

"I am PROFESSOR WONDERFUL, head of evolutionary research for Evolution, Inc. If you are one of God's sexy angels you are welcome, but keep God's damn Spidervater out of here. No bugs allowed on the forth floor. I can't stand them. You look great in our lab outfit, (A skin tight lab outfit with peek-a-boo breasts and pubic area) but who do you think you are? You almost scared our guard Hans out of his wits."

"I am agent 0069."

"0069! We've been expecting you. Give her another squirt. You can never be too sure of God's strong-arm persons. Most of them are lousy with venereal diseases."

Two attendants spray JUSTINA with a bug killer something like DDT. WONDERFUL goes down on the squeaky clean floor with a magnifying glass inspecting the results. He picks up something with tweezers.

"Ah ha. You see, you can't be too careful. A rare blue crab from Baltimore, Maryland."

JUSTINA is highly embarrassed. "Well, I never... I gave a ride to a horny rabbit on the way here. I must have caught it from him."

"I see. Must have been Noah's Ark Jimmy. He has two of everything on him somewhere. But the endangered blue crab, found only on the toilet seat in the men's room of the Gaiety strip club in Baltimore, Md. This is truly amazing."

JUSTINA recovers her sangfroid.

"Why don't you study them in their natural habitat?"

"I'm only fifteen MISS WANE."

"Is that too young to study toilet seats in strip clubs?"

"I have more important things to do. Have you seen our latest cockroach control device?"

"I'm here to see all the latest gadgets. My assignment is to turn the tide of sin that is sweeping the world."

"You're kidding? Wipe out fun?"

JUSTINA sternly admonishes WONDERFUL not to play with her.

"Don't play dumb with me."

WONDERFUL gives this profound idea a quick once over.

"You're right. It's impossible for me to play dumb. I broke the I. Q. meter at Cat House Tech.

"I thought that was a peter meter."

"You're right and it's for guys who have their brains in their balls. It was my first great invention and made me famous when I broke it."

"I thought you went to M.I.T."

"I did. Cat House Tech was just up the street. I went there on my thirteenth birthday to attend a seminar on safe sex and got the idea for my I.Q peter meter."

"You are a precocious little genius. But what have you invented lately?"

"We are almost ready to test our super nova bomb."

"Isn't that kind of dangerous? Where would you test a thing that awesome?"

"Someplace far away, like the La La Land Deli."

"I hope that's a few galaxies away PROFESSOR."

"Actually it's a famous Jewish Deli in what used to be the San Fernando Valley before it seceded from Los Angeles."

"But that'll take out this whole galaxy, won't it?

"Can you think of a better promotional stunt?"

JUSTINA is really pissed at WONDERFUL'S smart-ass joke.

"Let me remind you PROFESSOR WONDERFUL that I am here on God's business. Serious business. I want to see the latest secret weapons. No more jokes Mr. 15-year-old genius or you'll have to answer to SPIDERVATOR."

"Then you better come up with a better password than you came up with for Hans. Spiders don't scare me."

"Get your hand off my ass or die."

"That's it. Come this way MISS WANE. I want to show you how we have successfully harnessed cold fusion."

PROFESSOR WONDERFUL takes JUSTINA into a cluttered laboratory and shows her a Rube Goldberg sort of contraption that has a large hissing cockroach hooked up to it.

"What are you doing to that poor cockroach?"

"Splitting the atoms of its sperm of course. That is how we attain cold fusion."

Just then all the lights in the laboratory go wild and the cold fusion machine lights up like downtown Las Vegas, indicating fusion energy. At the same time it begins popping popcorn looking cockroaches like a popcorn machine.

JUSTINA is disgusted.

"Just what the world needs, cockroach popcorn."

Wonderful is scrutinizing a graph that shows the ratio of cockroaches produced to sperm inputted.

"We are only one or two cockroach pops away from achieving more cockroaches than sperm energy inputted. "

"I'm not impressed. A miss is as good as a mile. What have you got that I can use?"

"How about some of this instant hair on chest macho shampoo and shrink cream for camouflaging your tittees?"

"I'll pass on that. But if you got any mousetrap padded bras I'd be interested."

"How about this Komodo dragon poison gas flavored toothpaste milked from a Tock-Tock highway toll collector's fangs. Just brush with it each morning and you'll be known as dead eye dragon dick breath."

"I discovered that snake breath on the way here. Great stuff. Give me a dozen tubes of those. I'll be able to get a seat on the bus during rush hour from now on."

"And how about a set of these beautiful chrome knuckles?"

"Why chrome knuckles?"

"Color coordinated to ward off carjackers when you are undercover in our vintage Ford Thunderbird."

He pulls off a cover and there is a cherry 1959 Ford T-Bird.

"That's for me? Or should I say, that's for me!"

"Unless you prefer your motor scooter. This is a hand me down from GOD ZIMMER. It still has the original lightening bolt firepower. A little underpowered for modern mayhem, but your satellite remote more than takes up the slack. Now, instead of horny rabbits, you can pick up some real studs, like me."

"Yeah right, little dick. Got any special equipment?"

"Combo stun gun four speed vibrator with in/out around the world tilt seats and GPS auto drive star maps of the 100 top Playgirl centerfolds."

"Where's your mother? She should not only wash your mouth out with soap, she should drown you in maximum strength liquid detergent."

"I prefer bubble baths."

"I have to admit, you are doing a wonderful job here. But where do you get all your wonderful top secret ideas from?"

"Most of it comes from unclassified stuff in my school library and on the Internet."

"Well I guess you are living proof of that old saying, he who reads leads".

"In my spare time I'm creating my own universe. And it's going to be a beautiful garden world with real people in it."

"Isn't that idea patented by GOD ZIMMER?"

"That idea's obsolete. I'm going to offer fanatics 100 virgins for blowing themselves up. ZIMMER'S cheap. Who would blow themselves up for 70 virgins?"

"I can see there's going to be a lot of religious fervor in your world Professor Wonderful, but if everything is perfect isn't it going to be kind of dull?"

"On day three, I'm going to give everyone free will. By day four there should be full-scale carnage."

"Give me a hug PROFESSOR. It's been so wonderful meeting you. I got to go though. I've got GOD ZIMMER'S dirty work to do. I'll trade you keys to the scooter for the keys to that loaded T-bird. I could use a little flash."

Chapter 11.

JUSTINA Crashes Her T-bird

JUSTINA is cruising along in her vintage orgy of chrome T-bird with INCATROPOLIS in the distance. All of a sudden there is a tank coming the other way firing at her with its machine guns blazing. There is a Heidi blond female Nordic type behind the gun. JUSTINA loses control of the T-bird and it careens across the desert landscape and finally comes to rest in a tank trap. She is dragged out of her car by Indians on the warpath. The chief who rescued her from Alcatraz interrogates her. He wears a string of Mickymoto beads but is otherwise in male attire.

The CHIEF interrogates JUSTINA.

"How. Wow! Where you get this classic cherry T-bird? I saved you from nuthouse. You owe me one."

"What's going on? Your tank almost killed me just now. And that T-Bird isn't cherry anymore. Here. (Hands keys) You can borrow it if you fix it."

"My apologies. It was one of those damn trigger-happy Hessian mercenaries we hired to fight Evolution, Inc."

"We're at war? Who started it?"

"Evolution, Inc. offered us ten trillion in stock to merge Incaland with them, but we turned them down and they hired the Montana Militia to attack us. We countered by hiring the new female Fuhrer Gertrude and her Hessian storm troopers."

"Your whole tribe could get a makeover for ten trillion in stock. That's almost as valuable as a container ship load of beads in New Orleans during Mardi Gras."

"Not really. Shining Path Red Lip, Inc. stock is worth a quadrillion Evolution, Inc shares per share. That deal's a God Zimmer damn rip off."

"Gambling must be more profitable than gospel singing. You have enough money to buy the whole U.S. of A."

"If we don't have enough dollars, we buy some from North Korea 10 cents on the dollar."

"I love those Mickymoto pearls."

"I used to wear kind from Rocky Mountain oysters, but no one like."

"Since I'm a secret agent for Evolution, Inc., I guess I'm a prisoner of war. God pays lousy. You want to make me an offer to be a double agent?"

"Yes. How much to scalp you?"

"I'll save you the trouble even though that's in fashion now. Here, I'm wearing PROFESSOR WONDERFUL'S shape shifter wig. Fix my car and you can keep the wig."

The chief puts on her wig, looks at himself in a mirror and is much pleased, especially when he turns into an Indian princess. Suddenly there are the cacophonous sounds of crashing garbage can top cymbals and out of tune bugles signifying an attack on their position. The Evolution, Inc. Montana Militia army overruns their position. The HESSIANS run away and the Indians drive away in JUSTINA'S damaged T-bird leaving her to the mercy of the Montana Militia. ANGELO has joined the Montana Militia and is the officer in charge.

Chapter 12.

JUSTINA is Captured By the Montana Militia

ANGELO is in the uniform of an officer and is giving orders. When he sees JUSTINA he accuses her of being a spy for the Indians.

"What the hells going on here. Are you a spy for the Indians? I always thought there was something suspicious about you JANE."

"I am not JANE and how could you accuse me JUSTINA WANE of such duplicity? I got attacked by some blond bombshell from VALHALLA and crashed my new T-bird into this berm. I gave the chief my new red wig to satisfy his genetic urge to scalp me and he was going to fix the bullet holes and return my car. Now, you've ruined everything. The Indians escaped in my T-bird and I'll never see it again." She cries bitter tears.

"I'm not fooled by your crocodile tears JUSTINA. CAPT. FURBALL, I want her tortured until she admits her name is JANE. Tie her to an anthill and cover her with whipped cream."

"Please no. I hate ants. I'll do anything CAPT. FURBALL. I'll even burn my driver's license and refuse to sign traffic tickets."

CAPT. FURBALL who is an Idaho anarchist is much impressed.

"She sounds O.K. to me sir."

"Listen you dumb hick, this driver's license was issued in Scoobi-Doobi Land. That's where mud people crawling with blue crabs play hip-hop scotch for a hit on a crack pipe."

CAPT. FURBALL follows orders with a vengeance.

"Take her away and don't spare the whipped cream."

"You son-of-a-bitch ANGELO! If I had my remote, I'd fuck your ass..."

ANGELO swiftly retaliates.

"Gag her too."

JUSTINA finishes her threat.

"...To hell and gone."

JUSTINA is dragged away gagged & kicking.

Chapter 13.

JUSTINA is Rescued By the Indians

The CHIEF is sitting at his desk in an Indian gambling casino that night watching the lady boxers on T.V. when his lieutenant comes in with a box. The CHIEF wants a report.

"Find anything valuable?"

The LIEUTENANT doesn't think so, but how wrong he turns out to be.

Not really; just the usual ladies junk. Here's a T.V. remote. Isn't yours broken?"

"I'll check it out. Make sure she gets all this stuff back when we return her car ...fixed. We're not thieves. Let me see that remote a minute. Damn female boxer dikes. Don't know what the world is coming to. There's a good cowboy and Indian movie coming on."

The CHIEF pushes several buttons. Each time he pushes a button, a boxer is knocked out and an announcer with breaking news interrupts the program with news that another city has been nuked out.

"Damn! Just when the buffalo have returned and we're making a killing, those palefaces are nuking out civilization one city at a time. This remote is no damn good. And worse, every time I push a button another boxer is knocked out too."

Finally, his T.V. tube blows. The picture phone rings and Gertrude is on the line requesting that the Hessian mercenaries receive their pay. The Indian Lieutenant relays this to the Chief.

"Our Hessian mercenaries want to get paid sir."

"With soldiers like those no wonder King George went coocoo. Pay them in casino chips and *trick* them to play at the loaded dice table. I can't afford to pay losers."

The Lieutenant gives GERTRUDE orders.

"Meet me in the Casino in five minutes. (Hangs up) What are we going to do for an army chief, if the Hessians quit? Our situation is desperate."

"Go pay those bums and I'll have a plan when you return."

The HESSIANS march into the casino in formation. Their FUHRER is GERTRUDE with the blond pigtails and horned helmet. Right out of Wagnerian opera. The lieutenant pays the HESSIANS with casino chips. He hints they can win a motherload at the loaded dice table if they play. The HESSIANS pool their money and GERTRUDE rolls the dice for them.

"If you want to try your luck for a bonus motherload, the CHIEF guarantees craps table # 1 will bring you luck." (Thinking to himself, "bad luck")

"Soldiers of the Fourth Reich, ve Vill get rich. If ve don't vin, ve'll smoke these Kosher Indians and use them for rations."

The HESSIANS click their heels and give the Nazi salute to GERTRUDE.

"Heil Gertrude!"

GERTRUDE rolls the dice.

"Der Fadderland needs some new jack bootees."

GERTRUDE wins. The HESSIANS cheer. The casino lets them win a couple of times on small bets before it uses it's loaded dice to win all their money on the big bets. After they lose all their money, they start to shoot up the casino, but are surrounded by Indians in war paint that scares them off. The Indian lieutenant shouts at the mercenaries.

"Soldiers of the Fourth Reich. You are a bunch of losers. Losers must pay with their scalps."

GERTRUDE tells soldiers to be brave.

"Come soldiers of the Fadderland. Ve vill die like true Fascists."

The Hessians run for the exits. The CHIEF and his Lieutenant have a good laugh.

"I feel sorry for their next employer lieutenant. They couldn't win with C4 loaded dice."

"Chief that was our army. What do we do now?"

"You got the T-bird fixed?"

"Like new."

"Let's rescue JANE WANE. She can talk to her boss for us. Maybe we can make a deal. Half a loaf is better than no loaf at all."

JUSTINA is tied to an anthill. She has been saved from the ants by a thunderstorm. On the way to her rescue, the CHIEF beeps the T-bird horn at enemy sentries and lightning strikes them dead. The Indians are able to drive right through the hapless enemy camp unmolested and free JUSTINA.

The chief is pissed when he finds the palefaces are using his favorite anthill.

"Some nerve. Got you tied to my favorite anthill. Palefaces steal all Indians good ideas."

"Wait till I get that ANGELO. I'm going to boil his balls in oil before I get through with him. This rain is the only thing that saved me from the ants. How's my T-bird?"

"I'll be glad to give this T-bird back to you. The horn's got one hell-of-a bad short in it. The Great Spirit gets angry when you blow it and it speak with voice of thunder god. And this T.V. remote knocked out five female boxers and blew up my T.V."

"Chief, I owe you for the second time. Is there anyway I can repay you?"

"You know anyway we can get these palefaces off our backs? We want to run our casinos in peace."

"Give me that remote and take me to the Montana Militia encampment."

JUSTINA and the Indians are peering down on the Evolution, Inc. army encampment. She points her remote at the camp and clicks. Suddenly, SPIDERVATER appears and attacks the camp. She feasts on the EVOLUTION, INC. army. The tanks and artillery and other heavy weapons have no effect on SPIDERVATOR. Her laser eyes turn their heavy weapons into molten metal. She destroys the entire Montana Militia Evolution, Inc. army except for those who run away.

The CHIEF is mightily impressed.

"Wow. Where'd you get that dog with the groovy eyes? I'd like to get a couple of its pups and we'd never have to worry about the paleface again."

"I borrowed her from GOD ZIMMER, but he's going to be furious when he finds out I used her to destroy his army. We better vamoose. Come on. I'll drop you off."

JUSTINA and the Chief jump into the T-bird and take off.

Chapter 14.

<u>God is Really Pissed Off.</u>

In the penthouse of his skyscraper metronome, GOD ZIMMER has been watching these antics on mobile satellite T.V. from his drone flying TV camera. He is furious at both ANGELO and JUSTINA, not to mention BLACKIE.

"Thanks to this bumbling generation of secret agents, Evolution, Inc.'s bottom line has been set back practically to the Stone Age. I don't know what the world is coming too." He tries calling JUSTINA. "Calling Agent 0069. Calling agent 0069."

JUSTINA answers, "Agent 0069 reporting MAESTRO!"

"This is GOD almighty agent 0069. Report to headquarters immediately and if you see agent 666 bring him in too. Have him dusted with DDT first though. Hanging out with militia bimbos, there's no telling what he's caught."

"Roger boss."

JUSTINA cruises down the Tock-Tock highway towing BLACKIE who is having great fun on roller blades. She sees ANGELO hitchhiking in his tattered military uniform. He is terrified when he sees JUSTINA and BLACKIE and tries to escape, but is lassoed by BLACKIE who follows JUSTINA'S orders and places ANGELO in the car tied up and under arrest.

"JANE baby, I'm so happy to see you got away from those pesky Indians."

"Eat him Blackie!"

"JUSTINA! It's DR. MARCONI. Call off that thing or you'll be sorry. We still have a bet."

"I'm not finished with you yet ANGELO. We've been ordered to report to the shop. God's got his planet Goggle mobile drone surveillance on or I'd let BLACKIE snack you for lunch bet of no."

"Are you mad at me? That old abandoned anthill was just a joke to teach you a lesson about male supremacy. I was going to lick the whipped cream off you myself. Do you think I'd waste good whipped cream on ants?"

"You know what you are ANGELO. You're a coward and a liar and a pervert."

"That's the pot calling the kettle black. Add traitor to that list and the shoe fits you like a glove."

JUSTINA points her remote at ANGELO. ANGELO kicks it out of the car and lunges at JUSTINA. GOD is furious and sends the car crashing into a wormhole. SPIDERVATOR continues skating down the freeway with cars crashing out of her way. JUSTINA and ANGELO have the ride of their lives. When they come out of the wormhole, they find themselves in another country at war."

GOD ZIMMER has had enough of these two dangerous agents.

"Those two losers deserve each other. I've sent them where they can't do any more damage than has already been done. I've got a great replacement for them too."

Chapter 15.

The New Russian Revolution

A battlefield in Russia where the new Russian revolution is going on. In the center of the battlefield is a bullet scarred red electric organ with a body draped on it. There are two armies facing each other. The HESSIAN mercenaries led by

Gertrude are now fighting on the side of The Russian Mafia, Inc., that rules the country. ANGELO & JUSTINA are fighting on the side of the dissident revolutionaries trying to overthrow the criminal pseudo-democratic oligarchy. It is the second Russian revolution. JUSTINA & ANGELO who have been thrown clear of the Corvette are crawling around dazed looking for help when they butt heads.

"Ouch! Why don't you look where you're going ANGELO? And what daymare is this? I dreamed I totaled my T-Bird. And what are you doing in that general's uniform? Who promoted you? And I'm only a major?"

" Major nuisance you mean."

"Where are we? Why aren't we in a hospital after that crash?"

"You must have amnesia from the crash. This is Russia in the year 2020. We are fighting on the side of the dissidents who are trying to overthrow The Russian Mafia, Inc and bring democracy to capitalism."

"Oh, yes, of course. Now I remember. We are mercenaries for God. But where is our good friend SCRIABIN the musician?"

"Poor foolish SCRIABIN. All the Czars horses and all the Czars men would not be enough to put that dummy back together again."

"ANGELO, my dear, you are a lousy poet."

"I don't care what I am. I'm sick of fools."

"SCRIABIN a fool? A fool because he sacrificed himself for the future? For us? For mankind?"

"For self-serving indulgent heroism you mean?"

ANGELO, who is losing it, sustains a long maniacal laugh while JUSTINA criticizes him for his lack of loyalty to his friend's memory.

JUSTINA loses it momentarily in an in his face rage at ANGELO'S disloyalty to their friend.

"For GOD ZIMMER'S sake, ANGELO! Have you gone crazy? Don't you know the dead have ears? You rotten hypocrite of a turncoat traitor, SCRIABIN was your best friend. How can you laugh at his death so maniacally?"

"And comrade, is it not the first law of nature to laugh at those who do not follow one's good advice?"

"Love is the first law of nature. You my friend are fatally flawed."

There is machine gun fire and bullets whiz by.

"Down. Get your head down." He pushes her down and falls on top of her. "I love you. That Nazi machine gunner again. It's getting on my nerves. I wish somebody would kill the bastard."

"If you love me, why don't you do it and prove it. Talks cheap!"

"I do love you, but I outrank you. It would be dumb military strategy for a general to risk his life when there is a major to sacrifice."

"Not in your case ANGELO baby."

"How would you like to be raped for not obeying a direct order?"

"It would depend on who gives the order. In your case I'd rather be shot."

"I can't wait to beat you at your own game. I'm going to make you eat those words Jane."

"When I'm finished with you Angi, you won't have words to describe it."

There is more gunfire and explosions. ANGELO and JUSTINA who have drawn their respective guns dive for cover.

Chapter 16.

The Female Fuhrer

GERTRUDE and her HESSIAN mercenaries have hired on to fight for The Russian Mafia, Inc. GERTRUDE is a machine gunner ensconced in a very luxurious pillbox. It is mink lined and she has a box of chocolates next to her. She wears her horned helmet and a Nazi uniform. Her last name is ODIN and she claims to be the TEUTONIC goddess of warfare. She fires maniacally at any sign of life.

"My name is GERTRUDE ODIN. My rank is Fuhrer. My serial number is XXXU233. The U233 is because of my Lucky Pierre submerging expertise. When I say periscope up, it better go up or else. My friends call me DIRTY GERTIE. I am the androgynous goddess of warfare. It is my appointed task to receive and feast the too numerous to count heroes who have had the sacred honor of falling in battle. (Firing crazily) Hey! Whoopee! There's some dummy sitting at an electric organ. Let's see if he is on the manifest. (Thumbs thru ledger) Yep! There's his name. SCRIABIN! Pianist-composer-idealist. Oh boy! I'll get an Iron Cross, I mean Red Star, I mean Medal of Freedom, I mean... oh phooey, I don't know what medals they're giving away these days, but I'll get one for this fanatic. Says here, thinks he can raise the consciousness of the human race by getting all the musicians in the world to play the same note at the same time. He wants to drive everybody crazy." She laughs manically as Scriabin sustains a note on the red electric upright organ.

The musician SCRIABIN is sitting at a solar powered electric organ right in the center of a no man's land that separates the two opposing armies. After holding down a single note long enough to unnerve the undead, including GERTRUDE, he plays with a maniacal fury. GERTRUDE is furious. She fires her machine gun at SCRIABIN, riddling he and the organ with bullets, until he stops.

"Even though I am also the hermaphroditic goddess of culture, I still consider this unclassified music an affront to my duel sex organs. His poor mother; all the trouble he must have caused her. When will women learn that men are no good? And they're such swine they always die with an erection. GOD'S work is exacting. Sometimes I'd rather be home knitting little jackbootees. Ho hum. I must fill my quota."

JUSTINA & ANGELO are keeping covered in a trench taking turns looking through spyglasses at SCRIABIN playing the organ. Their hatred of each other has temporarily evaporated amid this unexpected turn of events. They dance and hug each other happy to see SCRIABIN is alive and able to give a concert. They try to get his attention as best they can.

JUSTINA is ecstatic because she is in love with SCRIABIN.

"He lives. He lives. Oh thank God. He is a genius for the ages. You see hypocrite, he lives.

"SCRIABIN! SCRIABIN my bosom buddy. Over here! It's your friends ANGELO and JANE."

Just now the firing by the HESSIANS begins and SCRIABIN and the organ soon look like Bonny & Clyde's car.

ODIN is passionately firing her machinegun at the wildly playing SCRIABIN until he screams in agony and collapses on the organ. The same single note, as at the beginning, is sustained as GERTRUDE smiles happily and pops a bon bon.

"That's what I call a good liberal."

The mood goes sour in the trench, as JUSTINA is crestfallen to see SCRIABIN'S fate. ANGELO is sarcastic and almost jovial to see that his predictions have come true.

"I told you. The damn fool finally got what he had coming."

JUSTINA is wiping tears as she sobs...

"Martyrdom?"

(Sarcastic) "Yeah, right."

"You're an incurable hypocrite Angelo."

"Damn this trench warfare. I'm sick of it. I don't think the world is worth saving. I'm disillusioned."

"Liar. You never had any ideals to be disillusioned about."

There is more machinegun fire and a death scream.

"Woof... Did you hear that one scream? It must have hurt badly. Another idiot dies to save the world."

"How did a hypocritical bastard like you get to be a general of the new world order?"

"What's the fucking use? I've realized that we're really fighting to bring back the old world order. We die if we fight and we die if we don't fight. It's all the same. Only the icons survive."

"It's a curse to live when there is a war to die for. War is death, if you haven't heard Angi."

"You're a terrible morale builder, you know that JUSTINA?"

"Better dead than living dead."

"I couldn't agree more."

"Then why don't you do something ANGI baby?"

"Why don't you? I order you too."

"I have taken more than my share of risks. You charlatan! You opportunist! You always succeed in getting someone else to take the chances."

"There you go whining again. Just like a woman."

"You bastard. I'm more of a man than you are and I'll show you one of these days."

"Shut up! I hear someone coming. It may be a commissar. Pretend you are shooting."

Chapter 17.

The Ghost of Leon Trotsky

A man approaches through the trench toward JUSTINA & ANGELO. He is wearing a Russian general's uniform and insignia, circa 1920. It is the ghost of LEON TROTSKY. He has an ax embedded in his head. He falls to the ground at the feet of ANGELO & JUSTINA. JUSTINA tries to help while ANGELO holds a gun on them.

"Sir! You have a grievous wound."

Trotsky struggles to his feet.

"Pay no heed children. One life means nothing when your country's life is at stake."

"Sir! Generalissimo. May I be so bold as to ask your name, rank and serial number? Regulations you know."

"Don't apologize. Spies are everywhere. I even suspect myself, but if you'll forgive me, I can't even remember my name."

"But Sir, everyone is suspect. This is civil war. Surely, if you can't give us your name, you can give us the password?"

"Password? Let me think for a minute. My memory isn't as good as it used to be. Oh, I remember now. A password is a word that allows you to pass. Yes, of course! It just came to me. Nilats. That's it. The password is Nilats."

ANGELO & JUSTINA respond simultaneously.

"Nihilist?"

"I said Nilats. (Spells) N-I-L-A-T-S. It's a beauty, don't you agree?"

ANGELO locks, loads, and aims at TROTSKY.

"I don't agree. The password is Stalin."

TROTSKY responds Like a Yiddish mama.

"So what do you think I said? Nilats is that bonehead Stalin spelled backwards."

"O.K., you got us on that one, but we still need to clear up who outranks who here. I am a general too, so don't try to pull rank on us because of your biblical age."

"Oh ye of infinitesimal faith. Words have the highest rank. They are the fastest bullets and swiftest fate."

JUSTINA puts in her two cents worth.

"Listen pop. This is no game we are playing. Cooperate or else."

ANGELO remembers the sexual game they are playing.

"Wait a minute JUSTINA. Have you forgotten our amnesia game? I get to screw you when I win JANE baby."

"Over my dead body. And Jane is dead. Just your type baby"

"I'm starting to like this game JUSTINA.

"You two are vicious. I will cooperate any way I can. How would you like to have my headache miss?"

"You can start by giving me that dangerous ax."

"I will never part with this ax. It's a gift from an anonymous admirer."

"Who wanted to help split your winning personality no doubt"?

"And keep his brains from falling out Justi."

JUSTINA & ANGELO high five their cleverness and convulse into paroxysms of laughter. TROTSKY is not amused.

"I would have you two shot, but you have cured my amnesia by your moronic impertinence. I am your commander in chief Leon Trotsky. While you sit here making jokes, you could be spreading the revolution abroad."

JUSTINA & ANGELO go into even greater paroxysms of laughter.

JUSTINA while laughing manages to blurt out,

"It is LEON TROTSKY. I've seen his picture in ancient zines."

ANGELO pauses long enough to digest this and starts laughing again.

"Ha, ha, ha. You're about 100 yrs. behind the times POP. The revolution has gone full circle and it's back in mother Russia again. Capitalist monopoly has taken over the world. We are fighting to free Russia from the yoke of capitalist cronyism and bring about a real New World Order."

"Yes, this one is as bogus as a three-kopek wet noodle."

"Let's stop talking and get on with it then you two backsliders."

"But he can't be TROTSKY, ANGI. An agent of STALIN killed him in Mexico. And with an ax in the head. You're a ghost."

JUSTINA & ANGELO stop laughing and look at each other as though they had seen a ghost. The chatter of a machinegun interrupts the confrontation. ANGELO & JUSTINA dive for cover, but TROTSKY fearlessly stands there as the bullets scuff up the nearby dirt.

"Aaah... The imbecile of war is chattering like an alarmed peacock."

"Down you fool. Get down. He must have escaped from an asylum."

"By my ancient ass get down Major. Charge! Attack! Destroy the defiler. Kill the infidel. I order you to show the enemy your pluck soldiers of the New World Order. You are the hope of mankind. What are you waiting for? General, I give you a direct order to order a full-scale attack. Major, in respect to your gender, you will have the honor of being the first over the top."

"I am only a pseudo female General. In the New World Order, everything is pseudo. There is no gender."

"Don't you want to be the first cyber hero to receive the first medal of virtual honor major?"

"This may be a war game General, but that is a real machinegun."

"It is only a real fear."

ANGELO who is paralyzed with fear finally chimes in.

"It is hopeless general. Do you want us to be killed for nothing?"

"Are you two totally without principles? You must believe in something?"

JUSTINA shows her true mettle.

"The world believes in pseudo capitalism, pseudo socialism, pseudo democracy, and a pseudo God. I believe in pseudo."

"I believe in humbuggering dead females."

"I shall have you both shot."

"We do not take orders from imposters do we ANGELO?"

"Or traitors."

"New World Order scofflaws and all counter iconoclastic devils that would turn the clock back to the Old New World Order, beware! By the authority vested in me as commander in chief of the dissident army of the newest New World Order, I order all soldiers and fellow evolutionaries to attack the corporatist Commies. As an example to posterity, I Trotsky will be the first over the top hero to challenge the ideology of greed crowing on yonder impasse."

ANGELO is much perplexed by TROTSKY.

"Is he talking in split tongues now? I can't understand him. What'd he say about over the top corporate commies? They're raiders of ancient bathhouses looking for lost gold teeth? Is he an evangelist from hell?"

"He said corporations are Communism dummy, as in socialism for the rich. Pop, you got almost original ideas, but when are you going to stop making speeches and show us that right over the top stuff?"

"I'll show you the right stuff. If some turkey shoots at you, gobble back. My patience is at an end with you two."

He charges over the top, gobbling like Sgt. York. "Gobble, gobble, gobble." He shoots a pop up HESSIAN who apparently didn't see the movie Sgt York.

GERTRUDE is sitting with a bored frustrated look on her face in her pillbox. She is popping bon-bons and reading Menschhouse Magazine. Finally there is a turkey call and TROTSKY is seen bobbing and weaving and shooting HESSIANS. He almost reaches the pillbox before ODIN is able to smoke him.

"Sweet Jesus. Why did I ever want to be the first female FUHRER and lead a bunch of bonehead mercenaries fighting for a free market? And these corporate Commies who run the market are a bunch of tightwads. All they pay is mercenary minimum wage, 99 bucks a hr. Hardly enough to keep me in bon-bons. Hey, what's that gobbling sound? A turkey? Yum, yum, and it's almost Thanksgiving too. There is a God after all. (TROTSKY is out of bullets. ODIN shrieks and shoots him) Wow, that was a close call. (Thumbing thru ledger) Can't find his name either. Poor old fool, he'll go to hell, because I had to make my own decision. Can't understand why everybody's so anxious to get to Valhalla. I'm no atheist, but I'm almost scared out of my Victoria's Secret boxer shorts that it might be a hoax. Poor ADOLPH. He would be so proud of me, even if I am working for non-Aryan cronies from hell."

The two malingerers watching through a periscope are shocked at what happens to TROTSKY.

"Do you believe what you saw? He wiped out half the Hessian army before that machine gunner got him. Thank God he's dead. That was a dangerous hallucination."

"How can you be so insensitive ANGELO? Have you lost all your humanity?"

"I'm still breathing because I've learned how to control my feelings. Life is a bad joke. If you learn to laugh at the rules, you will always be able to survive. Only people who are enlightened enough to make their own rules will survive this war. If you want to live, you must be amoral. The real enemy is conscience. You must find an anecdote for conscience."

"I hate you. Suppose everyone was as smart as you think you are? No one would ever oppose tyranny."

"Never fear, my dear. True believers are always in more than adequate supply."

"I'm not one, that's for sure."

Chapter 18.

God's Headhunter

ANGELO and JUSTINA see an almost naked Negroid man walking toward them across the battlefield. The man claims he is a refugee from New Guinea, but he is also a hit man for God. He is a headhunter and is still decorated in the fearful outward regalia of this group. He has an Afro, tattoos from head to toe, shrunken heads hanging at his side and his body is pierced with bones in various places. A loincloth and sandals are his minimal clothing and a stone-age ax weapon hangs at his side. He also carries an old fashioned cardboard type of suitcase with place pennants glued on it.

The HEADHUNTER is observing bodies lying scattered helter-skelter in the macabre design of modern warfare.

"They sure got some washed out looking dudes in this part of the world. I'll be glad to get back to civilization. It's like having nothing to eat but green apples when you haven't had a square meal in a week. I could be back home hunting those nice plump Indonesians who stole half my country. And this place is uncivilized. I just can't figure out why there's so much carnage. Everybody looks so well fed and they hardly ever take a head."

ANGELO AND JUSTINA see this strange apparition ambling in their direction. It is coming from no mans land and since no one is firing at it, they assume it is an enemy trick of some kind. TROTSKY killed most of the HESSIANS and GERTRUDE has fallen asleep. She has trip cans in her sector to wake her in case of a sneak attack, however they have no effect on stopping the headhunter from going about his business. ANGELO attempts to fire but his gun jams. JUSTINA is overcome with curiosity and cannot fire. ANGELO jealously sensing JUSTINA'S attraction to the headhunter urges her to fire her weapon at him.

"My God JANE! What in the world can that obscenity be?"

"Yeah... I see... Interesting..."

ANGELO tries to shoot, "My gun has jammed JANE. Shoot! Shoot! Shoot for God's sake."

"Hold it you fool. It may be one of our secret weapons. Let's see if he knows the password."

"I don't care. He looks like a sapper with that suitcase. Shoot! Shoot, before he blows us up."

JUSTINA smiles invitingly, "Halt there. What are you? Friend or foe?"

The HEADHUNTER is circumspect.

"Well, seeing as you got the drop on me, I don't think I got much choice."

JUSTINA still Smiling, "What's the password?"

"How about ten-inch stone ax?"

"My, my, he's heavily armed. Sir, can we discuss this in more intimate surroundings?"

"In church? I already have ten invitations to church picnics."

"This will be a real Holy Roller picnic. White turkey breast roll and designer stuffing in the outhouse."

"I prefer stuffing dark meat headfirst", licking his chops obscenely. "Or oysters Rockefeller on the Barbie."

"Kill the bloodthirsty obscenity Justi."

"Listen white bread. I haven't done anything to you ...yet. If you're hungry, there's plenty of fresh meat around here. (Pointing to SCRIABIN) There's one that looks tasty, if you don't mind white meat and he's still got a head."

"You want me to eat my best friend? This savage has no feelings. Shoot him before he gets hungry enough to eat white bread."

The HEADHUNTER is much mystified by the attitude of ANGELO and JUSTINA.

"Why's everybody so uptight? There's plenty for everybody. Gluttony's not very civilized you know."

JUSTINA tries to explain.

"There's a war going on. We do not kill people for food. We kill them just because they are people."

"Somebody steal somebody's wife or somethin'?"

ANGELO adds his two cents worth.

"The forces of freedom are battling the forces of oppression."

"(Dripping with sarcasm) "Which side are you on?"

"He's got his own side."

ANGELO expresses his opinion as insultingly as he can. He is trying to provoke a confrontation to give him an excuse to kill this rival, as he sees it.

"I bet you're on the side of the mother fornicators."

The HEADHUNTER drops a bombshell wake up call.

"I'm on God's side. I'm a headhunter for God."

JUSTINA & ANGELO look at each other mightily perplexed in alarmed amusement.

After thinking about it, JUSTINA is not amused.

"That's not funny. We work for God."

"Not anymore. You've been fired or should I say demoted major. I'm here to replace you. You too general."

"Oh, you're a hit man for God? And I suppose God's put a contract on us? (He has a good laugh) Listen boy. God doesn't send a boy to do a man's job."

"Boy? You think you're pretty funny don't you Porky Pig? Oink, oink, oink."

The HEADHUNTER opens his suitcase, which contains a nuclear bomb.

"I hope this small nuke doesn't spoil your day. It's set to blow as soon as I deliver it to the world's first lady FUHRER over there. If I were you, I'd jump in your battered T-bird and beat it out of here. It isn't your turn ...yet. But I'll be coming to see you... real soon."

JUSTINA and ANGELO are aghast. After the HEADHUNTER activates the bomb, he closes his suitcase and strolls away toward GERTRUDE'S pillbox. He intentionally trips the alarm cans to wake GERTRUDE.

GERTRUDE wakes in her pillbox when the alarm cans clang loudly. She is stunned at the specter she is confronted with and begins firing wildly before she has time to consult her ledger. All her firing is to no avail as the Angel of Death is immune to bullets.

"The alarm! I better get to work. Oh boy. Wow! Whoopee! Der Fuhrer should see my performance. I wonder where they get all the men? Dumb people must still have babies. What a waste of time. Hey! What's that I see coming this way? He's naked and he's black. I better check the ledger. Nope. Nothing fitting his description unless the Angel of death looks like a headhunter. (Laughs) I'm not fooled by camouflage. And this fools strolling along like he's on his way to a Sunday school picnic. Watch this. Even if he is the Angel of Death, I'll make him tap dance." She fires like crazy, kicking up dust all around the HEADHUNTER who doesn't flinch an inch. "Sweet suffering SAPPHO! This sucker can't dance." She frantically pores rounds into the HEADHUNTER. "Die will you? This must be a new bulletproof secret weapon. Oh, God help me. Maybe it's the Devil. Please God, I love you. Save me from this devil. Oh, oh, oh... (She runs out of bullets) God help me, I'm out of ammo. (Crosses herself and preys) Oh dear God, don't desert me now. (She rings up supply on a field phone) Praise the lord and pass more ammo quick. A non-Aryan angel of death is attacking me. There ought to be a law against this. I'm on my own." She slams down phone and starts to pray. The headhunter is almost to the pillbox. "Oh no, he's a Cannibal. I'm going to be crucified, roasted at the stake and eaten all at the same time. He must be with the Ku Klux Klan, but they're on our side." The Headhunter is standing over her, suitcase in one hand and dinner plate in the other. "Oh please sir. Don't hurt me. I'm just following orders and I'm too young to die. I'm a traffic cop for GOD. I take no personal pleasure in serving The Russian Mafia. God is my witness; I take no pleasure in all this killing. In fact, I teach Sunday school to holy roller-bladers."

The HEADHUNTER reaches the pillbox and stands there ominously until he speaks.

"Hey man, you know where I can get a foot long kosher hot dog?"

GERTRUDE points wryly toward the battlefield.

ANGELO AND JUSTINA are hunkering down in their trench watching the headhunter's progress. They also have put on dark glasses as a precaution. ANGELO ballyhoos the headhunter's chance of success.

"He got all the way to the pillbox. And the firing has stopped. He must be immortal all right, but all that stuff about a nuclear bomb must have been bull. New Guinea is still a Stone Age country."

"Not anymore. They have an alliance with North Korea."

The headhunter has dropped JUSTINA'S remote where she will find it. The crash has given her amnesia and she therefore doesn't know the deadly power of this remote.

"Look here. That savage was carrying a T.V. remote. I wonder what it is for?"

ANGELO goes pale with fear.

"Careful! It's..." (Too late)

JUSTINA pushes a button and the suitcase nuke goes off, blowing GERTRUDE to Valhalla. JUSTINA and ANGELO who are about a mile from the epicenter of the blast are blown off their feet, but are otherwise unhurt by this small nuke.

"Son-of-a-bitch. You got a bad case of amnesia JANE."

"Who me? And who is JANE? I am... I am JUSTINA WANE."

"Oh yeah... right. We're lucky to be alive. He was a suicide bomber for the devil."

JUSTINA cries bitterly, "I wish he had killed you. He was a man. I wanted him. I hate you, you faggot."

"Ah ha! You cry for blood and cry at the smell of death. Typical female inconsistency. Come here. Enough of this fighting. Let's kiss and make up."

"Stay away from me you pig. Oh God, I must be stupid. How could I have ever let you touch me?"

"I'm sorry JUSTINA baby. Maybe I have let my cynicism get a little out of control. You know I really am sorry to see SCRIABIN dead. I loved him more than I love myself."

"You think me a simple little fool?"

"Of course not. It's just that you're not very good at games."

"That's the truth, you charlatan."

"Without the benefit of my evolved level of consciousness, you would have been just another lamb led to the slaughter, like the rest of the suckers strewing this field innocent of their own folly."

"You evolved? You are an evolved liar ANGELO. You teach the same bullshit, as they all have since the beginning of the world. I'm out' a here."

"I won't let you desert evolution."

ANGELO draws his revolver. JUSTINA does the same. They then point their guns at each other in a mirror image. JUSTINA starts the indictment.

"You are chained eternally to rotting lies."

"You bimbo JUSTINA. You wouldn't know a rotting lie from an over ripe dildo. The naked crack of reality is..."

JUSTINA continues his thought, "...the new world order has brought back the old world order and you are its intellectual bonehead."

ANGELO takes aim at JUSTINA.

"Those will be your last words JANE."

ANGELO tries to fire, but his gun jams.

"Damn, my gun jammed! Kill me and end this game. It is the only way anybody will win."

"It must be God's will that we finish this game because mine won't fire either."

She keeps trying to fire for all she is worth.

Chapter 19.

Scriabin and the Lend lease American Nurse

Suddenly there is the sound of Scriabin's electric organ coming from no-man's land. SCRIABIN is playing his Hymn to Freedom at the battle scared electric organ. As he plays, JUSTINA and ANGELO forget each other and observe. As they watch, a Red Cross nurse appears seemingly out of nowhere. She wears a statue of liberty kind of toga that is transparent, and a Sister of Mercy's nurse hat. She cleans some of the blood and dirt off of SCRIABIN as he plays. Her name is PURITY LIBERATION. She is an idealist and speaks her mind.

"When in the course of human evolution, it becomes obvious that a mutational breed of men and women has emerged, finding their aspirations and beliefs in complete contradiction to that of their forefathers and the menopausal old men dominating the planet earth, it becomes inevitable that they must declare themselves independent of this foolish constraint."

ANGELO and JUSTINA are still confronting each other in a mirror image, guns drawn. They hear organ music and think someone other than Scriabin, who has been killed, is playing. Looking through their periscope, they see that it is Scriabin playing and that someone is ministering to him.

"Shoot me, shoot, shoot... I am tired of your kinky game Justi."

"You are the one who has been trying to tie me up. What's that music?"

"Maybe it's God's Headhunter learning to play the electric organ. If he has rhythm, it sounds pretty awful."

JUSTINA looking through the periscope askance describes what she sees.

"It's SCRIABIN and someone is ministering to him."

"Still alive? But the Mafia Commies riddled him full of holes."

JUSTINA is uncomfortably askance talking to ANGELO while trying to hold her gun on him and look through the periscope at the same time.

"And his organ looks like Swiss cheese too!"

" Where'd that nurse come from? They shoot prisoners on the spot."

"It must be a Mafia Commie trick."

"Use the sharpshooter scope to shoot them both, but save a bullet for yourself."

"You're a trigger-happy jerk Angelo. You're not going to win this game by the power of perverse persuasion, you bonehead."

SCRIABIN is wildly playing the organ with PURITY ministering to him. PURITY and SCRIABIN start to recite what sounds like a new bill of rights.

MISS PURITY begins the recitation :

"We hold these truths to be self evident; that every human being is endowed with certain inalienable rights; that among them is: "

SCRIABIN joins in, "Freedom from pseudo democracy".

PURITY continues, "That among them is:"

SCRIABIN says, "An economic bill of rights that will send overpaid corporate commie CEO's to the guillotine".

PURITY goes on, "That among them is:"

SCRIABIN goes over the top:

"Freedom to marry the object of your choice."

PURITY continues:

"That among them is:"

SCRIABIN responds, "The right to be outsourced with your job".

"That among them is:"

SCRIABIN is out of control:

"The right to health care, a job and a college education."

ANGELO and JUSTINA are jumping with joy that SCRIABIN is alive. The HESSIANS having apparently been killed by the bomb, they decide to take a chance on attempting to "rescue" SCRIABIN.

"He is alive. I'd recognize that dumb hymn to idealism anywhere."

"The HESSIANS are dead. Let's call medivac and get SCRIABIN out of there."

"Let's help him out ourselves. We'll be heroes JUSTINA".

JUSTINA & ANGELO race up to SCRIABIN & PURITY at the electric organ.

JUSTINA gushes effusively. "You are saved my love. You must come away from this awful organ massacre."

Scriabin responds with a wild phrase from his Hymn to Freedom.

"You're alive SCRIABIN. Your music may be for deadheads, but your organ playing is immortal?"

"(Sarcastic) I'm an immortal fool like you ANGELO, my... beloved friend."

"SCRIABIN, you of all people to call me a fool. But you are gravely ill my friend. Let us help you to a hospital."

"I am fine ANGELO. It is you who need radical surgery."

"For what?"

"For being a sophisticated blob."

"What you need my friend is a cultural lobotomy, because your Hymn to Freedom is a flop. Nobody cares anymore. The corporate Commies are calling all the shots and nobody cares."

JUSTINA chimes in.

"Don't listen to that perverted asswhole. He's MAO TSE TUNG in drag."

"Liberation from the constraints of pseudo politically correct enlightenment is natural perversion.. You and he are two drags in a pod comrade."

JUSTINA doesn't like this comparison to ANGELO. She goes thin skin ballistic.

"Freedom to hate."

SCRIABIN rubs it in, "Bitterness is a box with infinite sides my dear."

"You dare reject my perspicacious pussy?"

"Jealousy is counterrevolutionary. My organ recital will be available when you earn it."

JUSTINA is unrequited female fury. "Freedom to kill!"

PURITY tries to defuse this incipient antagonism.

"Man is created in the likeness of a creative GOD. God help us."

ANGELO'S take is, "We need cake and you ask for bread?"

SCRIABIN retorts, "Man deserves the best. Only a glue head lives by wonder bread alone."

JUSTINA is wide eyed wonderment, "Speaking of a wonder. Look what's coming. An ape in an Armani suit."

"I'm falling in love with you all over again JANE."

The HEADHUNTER appears dressed in flashy clothes and speaks to SCRIABIN.

"Freedom to do drugs! Have a cigarette Cool?"

"Only the dumb die young. I'll pass Fool."

PURITY tells it like it is, "They have polluted the air, the rivers, themselves".

SCRIABIN punctuates the following to music.

"This is the HEADHUNTER magic show folks. Do it all."

The HEADHUNTER has become a drug pusher.

"Got coke, acid, ice, ups, downs, all a rounds and if you got a yen for the end, ah got some heroin."

PURITY says, "They worship supply at the expense of demand."

The HEADHUNTER says, "I'm a turned on, tuned in funky monkey."

SCRIABIN says, "You look more like a stir-fried flunky to me".

"Hey now fool. Don't blame a simple headhunter for God like me." Pointing to ANGELO. "I'm expanding my consciousness. Homeboy over there helped me evolve from a headhunter to a bush clipper. Maybe I'll start eating wonder bread and turn into a loaf of glue like you."

ANGELO pipes in, "Look at the positive effect it's had on me."

PURITY continues to confabulate, "They are prodigal sons of rich cheerleaders."

SCRIABIN retorts, "While Shakespeare is collecting beer cans in the ally".

The HEADHUNTER makes nice and takes a head, "That makes him a headcanhunter, right bro?" He high fives ANGELO.

ANGELO dumps hard rock, "Not till he has to take a SCRIABIN." ANGELO high fives the headhunter.

JUSTINA pisses her pants with delight, "You mean he eats SCRIABIN and barks at the moon?" All three high five.

They all have a loud laugh at SCRIABIN'S stoic expense when they are startled by TROTSKY stumbling in sans the ax in his head. His brains are falling out of his wound.

PURITY goes medical, "Are there any forlorn, downtrodden or wounded here?"

They all raise their hands.

TROTSKY is all old folk complaints, "Oh my poor head and nobody has an aspirin. Not even that poor lady FUHRER who lost her heart to that HEARTHUNTER. He's evolution's deformity."

The HEADHUNTER pleads instant evolution, "Hey man. I'm reformed too. No ax see."

TROTSKY is unregenerate. "You probably stole mine and now my brains are falling out".

PURITY plays the sympathy card to the hilt.

"Oh you poor old man. What a grievous wound."

"What do you know of wounds you imposter?"

"I'm a sister of mercy from CALCUTTA."

"Calcutta! Don't make me laugh. There's no mercy in Calcutta. And I'd know a lend lease C.I.A. agent from America anywhere. What are your name, rank and serial number before I have you shot as a spy?"

"My name is PURITY LIBERATION. I am a simple bride of GOD and my serial number would crunch any computer known to man."

"You look more like the bride of Frankenstein to me, but if you're so pure, how would you like to be the cream in my coffee?"

PURITY shows her radioactive core, "How would you like a fat lip you dirty old Bolshevik?"

Just now there is machinegun fire and most of them dive for cover behind the electric organ.

Chapter 20.
The Murder of Scriabin.

ODIN is back in her pillbox that has been charred from the N-bomb. The new GERTRUDE is a product of latest instant cloning technology. ODIN speaks: "Thank the good lord for twenty-first century cloning technology. They can destroy our comfortable pillboxes, but they can't destroy us. Feels good to be back where I can give back something for the Old New World Order. Hey! What's going on down there? Looks like a weirdo convention. Must be pledging their lives, their fortunes and their sacred honors to the task of taking away my inalienable right to life, liberty, equality, fraternity and killing for the government of my choice. (Fires machinegun) There's a little wake up call from Dirty Girty you bleeding heart corporate commie hating traitors. Oh my. I don't know why I get my boxer shorts in such a bunch over nothing. I hate all this disorganized killing really. The only reason I put up with it is I am a eugenics dropout. We need quantity instead of quality because we tried the quality ploy the last Reich and it was a media disaster. We're are still on the side of mass entertainment even if there are still too many ill-bred people who would be better off dead than brainwashed by those rappers. Next big thing in entertainment will be a rap grand opera or maybe three rap tenors. Sopranos after I shoot their balls off. I do believe in the new world order even if it is bringing back every obsolete idea ever dreamed up. As long as there is Fascism for the poor and corporate communism for the rich everything will be normal. These corporate commies are the most normal people there has ever been and they got the world by the ozones. Let's see if I can whack some of those organ huggers." She fires at the group huddled around the organ.

ANGELO and JUSTINE are hiding huddled behind SCRIABIN and the solar power operated electric organ. The others ignore the hail of bullets as though it is nothing but harmless hailstones.

PURITY continues to confabulate, "In their pride, they have molested the truth and gotten re-elected for it."

SCRIABIN spins the latest news. "And Socrates was left holding a bag of hot air."

ANGELO bitterly resists, "Will somebody call Bull Busters to save us from all this pseudo intellectual rhetoric?"

MISS PURITY, not to be outdone by ANGELO'S sour grape jousts. "We are the holy warriors of a virtual real new World Order."

"Anybody want to buy my slightly used boomerang straight from the new war in Iraq?"

MISS PURITY loses it. "Hell you say! I'll take that boomerang and hit you along side the head with it."

JUSTINA lets go a blood-curdling scream, "SCRIABIN! He's been murdered!"

ANGELO and the HEADHUNTER leaning on each other's shoulders unleash a tsunami of crocodile tears.

"Oh, the poor chap. Boohoo."

JUSTINE tells it like it is.

"And with an ax!"

MISS PURITY goes into paroxysms of confabulation.

"Independent thought is a cardinal sin."

The HEADHUNTER affects deep concern.

"You don't say. Dear me! This is a tad gross you know. Who, who I ask you, who in this latter day of the World Wide Web, who could be so primitive?"

JUSTINE lashes out, "You, you barbarian. This is your obsolete low-tech style."

The HEADHUNTER pleads not guilty to JUSTINA'S slander.

"You've got to be kidding. The Stone Age went out at least 50 years ago. Besides what motive could I possibly have?"

ANGELO piles on. "The same motive you've always had. You're a low-tech low life cannibal."

The Headhunter's feelings are hurt.

"Nothing like fair weather race relations huh bro? I have to admit though; I do sometimes get a craving for liver pate."

ANGELO tries to be helpful. "I order mine over the Internet directly from Chinese prisons. You can Goggle the address, key word liver pate China."

HEADHUNTER way out front. "No chance. It's all been recalled bro."

JUSTINA cannot be appeased. "Sounds like an ebony and ivory conspiracy."

ANGELO and the HEADHUNTER together. (Pointing to TROTSKY) "Accuse him. His ax is missing."

TROTSKY jumps in and takes charge.

"Where's the murder weapon? I'll take charge here."

ANGELO imperially accuses Trotsky. "In his head where it should be. And it looks like your ax pop, so we can't lynch the nigger... this time."

The HEADHUNTER is very pissed. "Where I come from we lynch cracker snitches and then eat them. Anybody for lunch? I'm doing the barbi."

"Cool your jets you two. It looks like an old man's work to me guys. I ran the instant DNA check."

TROTSKY defends his age. "He was not killed by the generation gap."

MISS PURITY waxes pure Trotskyite poetry. "Generation gap is somewhere between the North Pole and the South Pole where love got lost."

The headhunter tries to leave. "See you all later."

TROTSKY demands an explanation. "Where do you think you're going Mr. number one suspect?"

"Somewhere around the equator dummy."

TROTSKY analyzes the crime for future episodes of CSI moon base.

"Nobody leaves here until I've completed my investigation. (Speech like) At this dangerous crossroads in the eternal order of things, there is a far more important thing to be concerned with than a simple murder. Our beloved comrade SCRIABIN is lying dead and horribly mutilated. The word pig has been scrawled on his forehead. One of those here among this little group has committed what most correctly could be interpreted as counterevolution. As in every crime of capitol degree, it is far less important for us to discover the criminal than it is for us to discover the motive. For in discovering the motive, we discover what is of inestimable value to future generations. Here, my friends and fellow dissidents, in all its insidious brilliance, is the emergence of the creative element that most often in the common man lies fallow. This seemingly insignificant act is in reality, the essence out of which the perfume of culture is extracted. It is originality and originality is evolution. And evolution is dangerous, because it is revolution. And since revolution must have a foundation in dialectics, the indubitable conclusion must be that this heinous crime must have had some cause transcending motive. Ah! Do I see a look of bewilderment on your faces? Off the record, since I am quite satisfied with my own conclusions, I shall attempt for those of you who are a little challenged to explain my childlike, if novel formula. Firstly, evolution cannot proceed beyond the synthesis resulting in diametrical opposites. Secondly, man in his unnatural progression toward physical nirvana has only succeeded in accomplishing the total atrophy of his ideals. Thirdly, since his government, the corporation he works for, the media and his gods are all telling him the same lies, he has achieved the illusion of freedom known erroneously as democracy. I can only conclude then, that this act was an act of premeditated unnatural evolution, an act so completely alien to any known logic, it must have been an act committed by a visitor from another planet at a lower order of evolution than even the island this Stone Age hit man is from. My opinion, in conclusion, is that we have among us just such a visitor. It only remains, comrades, for us to discover who among us is capable of an original thought. If this requires torture, so be it."

MISS PURITY encourages the culprit, "Rebellion against mediocrity is obedience to God."

SCRIABIN resurrects himself, "Give me entertainment or give me death".

TROTSKY is livid, "What fickle fart in the face of fate is this? You're dead. Are you trying to make me look like a demagogic fool?"

SCRIABIN waxes esoteric, "You sir are a frigid mermaid drowning in your own goo. Blow hard on your sail old man. A body that does not give voyage to a shinning Mandela of eternal truth is destined to be an eternal traveler over an endless sea of vomit."

TROTSKY starts to weep, "I'm crushed."

ANGELO commiserates, "Don't cry General. You are right. He's the spy. His Hymn to Freedom is original crap. It's alien propaganda. What's the password Mr. Spy for the phony boloney crony oligarchy?"

"Albatrosses of a feather hang together."

This explodes most of the group into paroxysms of hatred toward SCRIABIN and MISS PURITY who remains neutral.

They finally decide to torture and cook SCRIABIN and PURITY both.

Everyone chimes in together except for MISS PURITY. "Torture him, beat him, hatchet him into little pieces, cut off his genitals and serve them for happy hour. Cook him on a spit like a pig. He is a pig. The spy is a pig. He's the alien. Tie him up and torture him. Let's have a luau and barbi the pig."

PURITY does her neutral thing, "Man is born free, but is everywhere in spiritual chains."

All together again, "Roast her too. Tie them together. There'll even be enough pig to invite the HESSIANS. They love pig."

They are tied together to the remnants of a tree that has been hit by a shell. They gather firewood and place it around SCRIABIN and PURITY. A blimp flies over advertising, "GOD ZIMMER for President of Evolutionland, Inc." Suddenly Indians start falling out of the sky. Another blimp comes by advertising "GOD ZIMMER for President of The Russian Mafia, Inc." It now rains Chechens. Another comes by advertising "POTATOHAN for President of Idaho, Inc." and it starts raining animated picaninny looking potatoes.

SCRIABIN calls attention to the blimp's significance, "Look up fools. There's your New World Order. There's pseudo-democracy in action. Made of potato heads, by potato heads, for potato heads."

Chapter 21.
The Firing Squad Fires.

As everyone is looking up, there is the sound of a Chinese army charge with bugles blowing and garbage can tops clanging. Our would be cannibals duck for cover as a colorful graffiti covered tank pulls up flying a white flag. GERTRUDE pops out of the turret without her horned helmet. She climbs out of the tank looking like "HEIDI in WONDERLAND".

GERTRUDE ODIN becomes a convert to joy. "Hello duckies. If you thought Odin the Destroyer was going to sit up there in that upscale pillbox all alone, while you bunch of New Old World Order freaks were having so much fun torturing and burning each other for happy hour, you must be a bunch of neocons and old-fashioned liberals planning a merger. But don't be frightened. I'm not going to hurt you. I'm going to join you. I love you. Yesterday's funny bunny bull's eye is today's kissing country pie. I love everybody. Come out of those foxholes wherever you are. Evolution for everyone. (To Headhunter) Hip-hop over here Mr. Cannibal heart breaker and bring your heads. Peace is declared. (The headhunter still displays shrunken heads hanging from his spiffy designer suit) It's time to have a yam good peace. (To JUSTINA) Come on JANE WANE, macho lady extraordinaire; let's have some fun. Sex is the ultimate weapon, as you know. (Bowing to TROTSKY) Oh great white father of revolution, I see you hiding there. Come on out of that foxhole and get on one more harder for humanity. This has been declared New World Order peace and orgy day. (To ANGELO) And there's the mad bomber in all his insane glory. Come out of your closet and blow up some minds. Evolution now! (To SCRIABIN) And there's the Messiah who won't save us, because we don't take his advice. Say something somebody. Let's have an old-fashioned country hoe down. (Starts calling) Grab your partner do-si-do."

GERTRUDE dances with TROTSKY, JUSTINA with ANGELO, PURITY with SCRIABIN and a female HESSIAN soldier with the HEADHUNTER. They are having a great ole hoedown when there is the sound of marching feet on a road leading into no-man's land. A squad of soldiers from the merged corporations of THE RUSSIAN MAFIA,

INC., INCA, INC. and POTATOHAN, INC. now called R.I.P. OFF, INC., march up to the group. Corporate Commissar JACK STALIN III leads the squad. The company is a subsidiary of NEW WORLD ORDER INC, which is controlled by the holding company EVOLUTION, INC., GOD ZIMMER, CEO. The Commissar declares the eight dancers enemies of the people and has them shot.

COMMISSAR STALIN marches his troops, "Hup two three four, hup two three four, hup two three four. Squad halt! What's going on here? What do you think you are doing? Don't you know you are under God's orders to kill each other? I must place you all under arrest. I COMMISSAR JACK STALIN III, by the authority invested in me by the merged countries of THE RUSSIAN MAFIA, INC., INCA, INC., AND POTATOHAN, INC., now renamed R.I.P. OFF, INC., a subsidiary of NEW WORLD ORDER, INC., a subsidiary of the holding company EVOLUTION, INC., condemn you cowardly dissidents..."

TROTSKY interrupts fearlessly, "Vy, you dough headed donut, I punch you right in your big corporate commie mafia mouth".

"Shut your face traitor! All dissidents are sentenced to death for daring to rebel against EVOLUTION, INC. We do not need you or want your unnatural selections. There is no profit to be made out of homeless lazy dissident swine. Firing squad, attenchut! Get ready, aim, fire!"

Everyone is shot down.

Real bullets have been banned in this future world as a wasteful misuse of human talent. People are shot with tranquillizer darts like animals. People captured in this way are made slaves and recycled into the system as zoo exhibits, theme park workers or other slave labor type of jobs. Thus and so JUSTINA is revived and sent on her way as once more the unwilling minion of GOD ZIMMER.

Chapter 22.

The Tacky Tock-Tock Highway.

JUSTINA is driving down the Tock-Tock highway in her T-bird toward the giant metronome in the distance. She passes many billboards advertising events, places and people in the now strip mall developed Evolutionland. Some of the billboards are:

1. "Fill up at Evolution, Inc. Service Centers. Lead for your pencil, gas for your ass. Highest achtum rating in the New World Order, Inc."

2. "Fly Evolution, Inc. Airlines. Frequent flyer implanted Angel Wings and touch tone genitals free after ten trillion miles."

3. "GOD ZIMMER Zoo. Best collection of two legged animals in Evolutionland."

4. "Evolution, Inc. Hot Dogs. Made with 100 % kosher pork blend."

5. "GOD ZIMMER is the old, new and in between Messiah. Paid for by the committee to re-elect God."

6. "Harley-Zimmer bikes from hell. Why stop for red lights when you can buy a bike that folds through wormholes a billion times faster than the speed of light?"

7. "GOD ZIMMER unified field theory Supermarket. Our string theory cheese is the only totally recyclable garbage in the known universe."

8. "Zimmer-Elvis Inc. Heartbreak Resort Hotel. Uncommitted couples only. Room comes with robot pubic shaves and all-purpose Zimmer Douche, mouthwash and hair-restorer. Free Gideon hell maps in every drawer."

9. "Zimmer-Mustang Dude Ranch Church. Buckingest fillies east of the Virgin paradise. Bilingual Sunday church services in Polish & Polish."

10. "Potatohan for President crucifixion memorial. Zimmer Life Support Systems for sale on the site."

11. "For the most evolutionary lips in the world wear Red Lips Stalin vaginal lipstick, a product of Zimmer-Gross Enterprises Inc."

12. "You are now entering ZIMMERVILLE; clothing and masturbating in the street optional. Tricycle speed limit mach 2."

JUSTINE passes the last sign and turns off at the POTATOHAN exit.

JUSTINA thinks out loud, "My. This place has evolved. It's just like America used to be. I want to see this memorial to SENATOR POTATOHAN."

JUSTINE takes the exit marked POTATOHAN MEMORIAL and pulls up to a man crucified atop a small hillock. It is not a statue, but a living man on life support systems. There is a sign that says, "Cavalry Hill", as opposed to "Calvary" where Jesus was executed. POTATOHAN is attached to a host of wires and tubes going to various parts of his body. There is a veritable circus surrounding him with all sorts of hawkers selling relics of his toenail clippings and other things. There is an arrow sign nearby that points the way toward a zoo with cages that contain people, as well as animals. It says, "Zimmerville Zoo Theme Park" This is really a concentration camp inhabited by political prisoners on exhibit in cages who have been captured for various crimes against the state such as in the preceding Russian civil war. This cruel and unusual, but profitable privatization idea has made prisons a paying proposition dear to the heart of the corporate culture that owns the country.

JUSTINA says hello to the senator. "Senator Potatohan! How are you doing?"

POTATOHAN actually can talk. "I could be doing worse. I could be off the government payroll."

"But wouldn't you rather be an entrepreneur?"

"I tried for president and got trampled. That's how I got here. I'll be lucky if they don't pull the plug on me. These pan vital organ life support systems have bankrupted the Federal Reserve System two years in a row, but the board of governors is taking the long Jap view. Or is it the short jump shot view? Whichever, I can't keep up with economic fashions any more. Everybody's going to be on these pan life supports in not very many years, so this is tolerated as necessary P.R. to create a great new market."

"But how did you get so sorely battered? You look like you were run over by a herd of wild horses."

"More like wild asses. I ran for President on the Great American Individualist Free Enterprise ticket and got run over by the press, which labeled me a commie rat."

"You poor man. The press got their labels backwards as usual. You must have stepped on some corporate commie toes. How did you ever get into politics in the first place?"

"I wrote a cookbook called, 'Living Like a King on a Potato a Day.' It made all those poor people who are always grumbling feel better and they voted for me."

"That's great. You're a Populist with a real program. What are you doing for an encore?"

"Writing another populist book. ' Living like a king on a rat a day.' Here's my prototype meal now."

An attendant wearing a MacRatBurger uniform brings Potatohan a MacRatBurger (A rat on a bun) from Zimmer's MacRatBurger Heaven that coincidentally has Red Lip arches similar to the Macdonald's kind. He takes a bite out of it. JUSTINE almost barfs and leaves.

"Hang in there POTATOHAN. You may be President yet. There are worse things than eating rats."

Chapter 23.

<u>The Evolutionland Zoo.</u>

JUSTINE pays the $50.00 entrance fee to the Evolutionland Zoo and takes a walk around. As people are its inhabitants, the Zoo appears to be only a euphemism for prison. She finds that for the most part, it is only ordinary people who have committed minor infractions that are incarcerated. However, they still for the most part have life sentences. The whole purpose seems to be to make money with the least effort and expense. Thus, there is not much turnover. The really big criminals are given important jobs such as corporate executives, judges, commissars, politicians or other important jobs. JUSTINE comes to a cage with a man in it who was a taxi driver.

JUSTINE interrogates this forlorn soul. "Sir. Why are you incarcerated in this zoo?"

The TAXI DRIVER talks, "I had three strikes against me."

"Oh dear. You must be a hardened criminal. What did you do?"

" I had two parking tickets in a wormhole and one for going warp 1 in a warp 2 tricycle zone."

"Oh dear. How long is your sentence?"

"I'm a lifer."

"Oh you poor man. Maybe I can help you get out."

"No, please. I like it here. We get three round meals a day. People on the outside are lucky to get one."

'I've heard of square meals, but what are round meals?"

"Freedom Fried round potatoes and a yummy Zimmer MacRatburger on Sunday. Free entertainment too. The Hairy Ainu Cheesecake Band gives us a free concert every Sunday afternoon. That's today. Why don't you stay? Visitors are welcome. And the value pack lunch is a deal."

"Those value packs are usually a rip off."

"Not this one. You get three round freedom French fries the size of   quarters and a double MacRatburger for only twenty dollars; Ketchup only a dollar extra; a glass of water and salt free, three refills."

"Yeah, that sounds too good to pass up. What did you say your name was?"

"Washington Jefferson Lincoln."

"I'm Jane Wane, AKA secret agent 0069. Nice meeting you and enjoy the rest of your stay. I just hope for your sake the French don't figure out how to genetically modify potatoes to the size of peas."

JUSTINA continues to wander thru the zoo that is a little bit prison and a lot nuthouse. She stops to see a kickboxing match between a male chauvinist and a women's libber. They fight a no-holds-barred physical match and taunt each other between blows. GOLDA GOOSEFINGER the GREAT and PETER HEADSUCKER the HARD are the opponents. These matches are for the benefit of the visitors whose entrance fee entitles them to be entertained in this theme park prison. The boxing ring is on the side of an alligator pit full of hungry gators just waiting for lunch if there is a false step by these killer kick boxer gladiators.

This is a world championship match for the mixed gender kickboxing championship. The announcer announces: "In the match of the century, we have in this corner, the world's female HEAVYWEIGHT boxing and man hating champion, GOLDA GONADGULPER GOOSEFINGER, the GREAT, undefeated in 150 matches of mixed gender boxing." A cheer goes up from a section of transsexual fans that were former male opponents of Golda. The announcer continues: "In the opposite corner, the world's HEAVYWEIGHT male supremacist boxing champion, PETER HEADSUCKER the HARD, undefeated in 150 matches against women, mostly in their third trimester. This match is sponsored by the World Male Supremacist Boxing Association. It is a fight to the death. The loser is gator bate."

The bell sounds and the fight begins.

PETER provokes Golda big time. "What have you got against an equal rights amendment for three-balled white males?"

GOLDA really passionately hates three balled men. "They're chauvinistic greedy slobs who get the best-lookin' chicks and I'm jealous."

"A gonad gulper and muff diver too? So that makes you bi-surgical?"

"You got that one right urinal sucker."

GOLDA lands a one two punch and a kick in Peter's genitalia.

Peter screams in pain. "You kicked me in my libber lubber liquorish stick you ingrate".

GOLDA taunts PETER, "Did you enjoy that lick Headsucker? Tell me, what is so great about head sucking?"

"The truth about head sucking will set women free."

GOLDA agrees, "Only if she wants to find out how many flavors of vomit men come in."

PETER punches and kicks her in her great ape implant transplant hairy chest. "I hope that was as good for you as it was for me."

"Oh, ecstasy! You pinched my priceless million dollar per punching bag tits, you Gatorades guzzling tri-balled pervert and it gave me an orgasm."

"I'm so sorry. I mistook your punching bags for pygmy pimples and wanted to massage them to pus."

GOLDA grabs him by the balls, "An' I got you by your three balls, Dickwart".

He has her by her nipples and she him by the nuts. They are both screaming and yelling foul in pain. The referee breaks their clench and warns them about fouls and foul language. GOLDA and PETER take him by the arms and toss him to the alligators.

"That entertainment was for wife number lucky seven who is at home listening to her macho man on her mold of my penis vibrator radio."

"She's probably home sitting on a big blackened Cajon cucumber like any smart housewife married to a shrink balled steroid junkie like you."

"You should know. I hear you sing the Lucky Pierre part in black church choir operas."

"You're just jealous. Black men and white woman are hauling coal to create a new master race."

"You'd steal the gravel out of Gravel Girty's asshole just to watch her asshole fall out."

"And if it did, it would be an obsolete white male like you"

"Listen you Velcro licking Bimbat, why don't you pogo up an elephant's asshole and have some hemorrhoid moose for desert?"

"You Tyrannosaurus twat of an atavistic asshole. You dirty twerd-eating turd. You hex on Rex. Go fuck a horny toad and jump up a dead dog's ass."

"You breach abortion dingle brat scraped from the rotorooted asshole of the world's champion butt banger, get ready to be shredded gater chow mein."

"Listen up urinal sucker. Tuck your pusbrained bigotry up your vampire asshole vagina blowhole. You are about to be genital wart gater snack, you micro-mini prick."

"You feeble fake fissure of a head fuck, I'm going to fracture your fascination once and for all. You're nothing but a diarrhea mouthed wonder warp of wasted words. A fart in the face of puffery has more sizzle than your finger fucking triviality."

"Listen up Halitosis Belchbrain. I diagnose your illness as terminal spermitosis. You're nothing but a bastion of bad breath come from eating too many sour grapes and before I get through with you, you'll be pulling your pud from a bad case of post-mortem praecox."

JUSTINA becomes ill listening to this bad vibe debate, "This entertainment is giving me a bad case of Macratburger heartburn. Why fuck up the gators? They should feed you two bad vibe champions to your fellow hyenas." (She splits)

PETER is pissed at the walkout, "Another aids bag critic? She must have had one too many Zimmer MacAidsburgers."

"I think it was your wife in drag."

"More likely it was your good fairy lick mother of the south."

Golda dives for Peter's gonads and snaps off his third ball. He screams in pain and delivers the next high-pitched line directly to the TV camera.

"Don't worry honey. I'll be home soon with two berries intact."

They now fight furiously and both fall into the alligator pit. The alligators want no part of them, however, and sprout wings and fly right out of the pit and head for the exit. The media headlines proclaim, "Instant evolution. Gaters sprout wings and fly."

JUSTINA walks up to a band pavilion and takes a seat in the front row near the punk rock band playing. The band is the Hairy Ainu Cheesecake Band. They are nude except for fig leaves and hair of which they have a lot. The lead singer is Ainu Annie. Some of the songs JUSTINA hears are "Cunty Honey", "Tap Tap, How's Your Sap"", The Rack & Pinion", "The Coffin Stomp," "Tortured For You", and last but not least "Hymn to Slavery". The song lyrics heard by JUSTINA are as follows:

Cunty Honey

Gnome, Gnome
I don't need no underwear
I don't need no underarm hair
I got a lot a cunty honey
And my honeycomb is sweet for you

Gnome, gnome
I don't need no raspberry douche
I don't need no pretty pooch
I got a lot a cunty honey
And my honeycomb is a hive for you

Gnome, gnome
I don't need no ring in my tittees
I don't need to sing pretty
I got a lot a cunty honey
And my honeycomb is home to you

Gnome, Gnome

I don't need no day glow bush

I don't need no tattoo on my tush

I got a lot a cunty honey

And my honeycomb is sweet to chew

Gnome, gnome, I want to moan

Gnome, gnome, I want to bone

While you guard my burning bush

Gnome, gnome, I want to moan

Gnome, gnome, I want to bone

While you guard my burning bush

Tap Tap, How's Your Sap Chap?

Tap tap, how's your sap,

Tap tap, how's that sap?

Is it rising yet?

Tap tap, is it hard as amber yet?

How's your sap chap?

Send it in the mail

Don't you fail

Tap, tap, I want some sap chap

Make the sap rap chap

So I'll take the crap

Send it in the real mail

So we can impale on a tail

Tap tap, I want your sap chap.

Erection, erection, erection...

Hard as amber

Hail to Unnatural Evolution

The Rack and Pinion Sic Heil

Torture torture torture Sic Heil

Uday, Souday and Posay

  Used to be your fans

Till they met their taker

The devil and his baker

This is good clean fun

Tear the Scum, Sic Heil

Hail to free body piercing

The Rack and Pinion hail

Hail Saddam and his sadist sons

On the gallows it was fun sic heil

His head rolled with a bow

And a fearsome rich man's scowl

Hail to unnatural evolution.

It's the ultimate solution Sic Heil

The Coffin Stomp

Can't get out this coffin bang bang

Can't get out this coffin bang bang

Eternity is a dick

When you have love handles on your prick

Can't wait to do the coffin stomp

Stomp stomp, bang bang

Can't wait to do the coffin stomp

Eternity is to snug for me

And ah gotta pee

Open up this coffin quick

Eternity is to snug for me, bang bang

Can't wait to do the coffin stomp

Eternity is to snug for me and ah gotta pee.

Chitti chatti pee, pee.

Chitti chatti pee, pee

Bang. Bang pee pee

Hermaphrodite Jew

I'm torn and tortured for you

And if I had a heart,

It would be bleeding too.

I'm twisted into a pretzel

All for love of you

I have chopstick eyes

I have Fuji apple pies.

In the tawdry blue night

I give kinky lessons in love

Can you spare a screw

For a hermaphrodite Jew

Life is a battlefield

A burning lake of liquid fire

He who laughs at the rules

Lives to fight another day

To weigh heavy on the world

Adorned with ten pound tit rings

Hanging like Buddha's balls

He has a chain link prick,

Ten feet of stretched steel

I'm twisted into a pretzel, for you.

Can you spare a screw,

For a hermaphrodite Jew?

Hymn to Slavery

Oh great God Zimmer,

Hallowed be thy name

Let us not take it to be vain

Praise be to your generosity

Praise be to your value meal

MacRatburgers are the rage,

Even when they give you aids

How like your image are we made

Full of greed, envy, pride and hate

Lust loving, like you are we made

Hallelujah the lord of jokes has come

Run and get your gun,

The NRA has its way with you

Hallelujah for bars and chains

God Zimmer is a dame

MacRatburgers are a dime a feel

Cockroach popcorn is almost free

And ketchup only a dollar a pop

Salt and pepper free

Hallelujah the lord of jokes has come

Hallelujah for French fried round potatoes

Hallelujah for Aids flavored meat

Hallelujah the lord of hell has come

And has lots of sex appeal

To a cross eyed seal

Sic Heil!

JUSTINA is a touch sarcastic, but not enough to be offensive, "Great material. Who writes your songs?"

AINU ANNIE does the talking for the band.

"GOD ZIMMER of course."

JUSTINA is a bit impressed, "You must be well paid working for God?"

"All the cockroach popcorn we can eat. Want some?"

"I'm a little full. I bought a dozen MacRatburgers to go. They were so delicious I ate half of them. You and the band can have the rest."

"No thanks. I don't care for aids flavored pork."

JUSTINA starts to retch and runs away. She passes a cage with a very fat ballerina trying to dance. The cage says, "The Gertrude, captured in Russia while leading a group of unnatural selectors in battle against the forces of freedom."

JUSTINA tries to be friendly. "Haven't we met before?"

GERTRUDE gives the wrong answer, "You look sort of familiar. You ever been an army dike?"

"Not that I can remember. Were you in the army?"

"Big time, but I got captured. Now I'm in one of those government-retraining programs that guarantee you a job."

"If you believe that, you must have fallen off a turnip truck and hit your head."

"You don't have an extra foot long wiener do you?"

"Sorry, I don't have one, but you can have the rest of my MacRatburgers. They're made out of aids flavored pork, you know."

"As long as they're Kosher, I love them. May the Fuhrer bless you my dear."

"I'll pass on that, but if you can tell me how to get to Evolutionary Headquarters, I'd appreciate it."

"That's easy. Just get back on the freeway and take the next exit. Say a good word to God for me. He pardons everybody from what I hear?"

"So I've heard. Listen GERTRUDE, I'm sure if you keep eating those MacRatburgers, you're going to lose a lot of weight and become a great prima ballerina. I can't wait to see your first performance. Keep praying to Saint Adolph. You'll probably be the first 300 lb. ballerina FUHRER in history."

Chapter 23.

JUSTINA Nukes Metronome Records.

JUSTINA is driving down the TOCK-TOCK highway and turns off at the Evolution, Inc. exit. She drives up to the Metronome Records entrance of Evolutionary Hqs. and parks. She goes into the lobby of Metronome Records.

JUSTINA walks around the lobby pushing elevator buttons and shouting for SPIDERVATOR. SPIDERVATOR finally comes down, but does not seem friendly this time and JUSTINA panics. JUSTINA barely escapes her clutches escaping out of the lobby.

JUSTINA jumps into her car and takes off. Red lip hounds from hell pursue her. The face of GOD ZIMMER sometimes replaces the heads on the hounds. This becomes something like an L.A. car chase in Disneyland. Cops in cars and on motorcycles chase her through Evolutionland until she is finally captured and turned over to SPIDERVATOR. All her worst nightmares come true. SPIDERVATOR brings her, car and all, back to the metronome. She is then brought to GOD ZIMMER who is in a bad mood.

"Good work 'BLACKIE'. Lunch is on AGENT 0069 today."

"What is the meaning of trying to scare me to death?"

"So you thought you could get away with becoming a double agent JUSTINA?"

JUSTINA is still at the top of her game. "My name is JANE WANE, God sir."

"Not any more JUSTINA. You are a disgrace to JANE. She was a stone cold killer. You are a wissy bleeding heart."

"I'll show you who is a wimp." She takes out the remote and pushes a button. There is the rumble in the distance of a nuke going off. "That was the national aquarium where you like to feed live political prisoners to the piranhas."

ZIMMER dripping with lethal sarcasm sneers, "I'm impressed. You're still a loser though, because you'll never forget you are a bimbo bomber named JUSTINA. JANE'S dead. You're a loser."

"You are wrong. I have evolved into a new person. True amnesia is to slough off your old self like a snake sloughs off his skin. This is what evolution is really about. You have sloughed into a monster. I have sloughed into a monster killer."

"Who have you become then?"

"I am JOHN WANE."

GOD ZIMMER gets a mighty laugh out of this. "Well big JOHN, consider yourself immaculately raped and impregnated. See him to his car BLACKIE! And if you get hungry on the way you may have JOHN WANE'S immaculately impregnated messiah fetus for a nice snack. From the inside please. I can't stand competition."

Another big basso laugh emanates from ZIMMER that segues into an insouciant female laugh and male God turns into a female Hindu Goddess type with all the extra arms, as JUSTINA and SPIDARVATER leave.

SPIDERVATOR, AKA BLACKIE carries JUSTINA uneventfully to the lobby. When they get to the car JUSTINA takes a box of bon bons from seat and gives one to BLACKIE. After a couple more bon bons, they soon renew their old comradely relationship. JUSTINA drives the T-Bird into the metronome's lobby and leaves it there. She then mounts BLACKIE again and they go rollerblading gaily down the Tock-Tock highway popping bon bons together until the metronome is a distant vision. JUSTINA takes out her remote and pushes a button. There is a mushroom cloud characteristic of an atomic explosion and the metronome disappears into vapor. JUSTINA AND BLACKIE take off pursued by apparitions of GOD ZIMMER and his hellhounds in hot pursuit. She starts to laugh hysterically. This segues to JUSTINA laughing hysterically in a padded cell in a hospital back in San Francisco. She is in a straight jacket alone in the cell until Dr. Marconi shows up.

Chapter 24.

<u>JUSTINA in a Padded Cell</u>

DR. MARCONI enters the cell, "Hello JUSTINA or is it JANE yet? I hear you claim to have been raped by God. There isn't any evidence to support this rape claim although it seems your claim to be a pregnant virgin has been verified by independent examination. I will give you a second opinion. And my opinion is final. Now then, are you another victim of the Immaculate Conception syndrome? Great excuse to stop from being stoned to death in some places, but who cares anymore in America? Tell me all about it?"

"You're making fun of me. She screams. I was raped I tell you. And by that Red Lip monster who claims to be God. Yuck! He had those huge red lips right up in my face. I loathe him and this evil world he's created. There's no way I'm going to be one of his immaculate conceivers either. This baby Jesus is going to be an abortion. Thank goodness for democracy that gives me a choice or I would rip it out of my body with my bare hands."

"Easy, easy. God has even bigger ears than red lips and his appetite is insatiable. Calm down. It's me ANGELO here with you. You're going to be O.K. JANE. The date rape drug somebody gave you will not kill you."

JUSTINA calms down enough to get her presence of mind back and demand they continue the game.

"Get me out of here. We have a game to play."

"Right." ANGELO has secured her release already. "You are free to go with me. And we're leaving for a Russian Mafia, Inc. controlled part of Russia on the next flight. They are lending us a space shuttle."

Chapter 25.

The Space Shuttle.

ANGELO and JUSTINA are taken to the airport in an ambulance. They fly to a central Asian space launching facility where after a lot of formalities they are escorted to a space vehicle. JUSTINA-JANE WANE is strapped in the seat of what looks to be a space shuttle. ANGELO is sitting strapped in next to her working a console with a joystick. There is a countdown to a launch going on. The Golden Gate Bridge is on the console's monitor. That is the target and the two of them will fly the shuttle there and crash it into the bridge as some kind of statement that the U.S. can no longer bully around the world. At least that is ANGELO'S plan A. They remain strapped there throughout the flight, never missing a beat in their competitive repartee.

"I don't think this is a great idea ANGELO."

"The Russian Mafia, Inc. group has been good enough to help make my greatest dream come true, and you think it's a bad idea? We're going to show the world the era of the bully is over. Anybody that wants to give America a lesson in humility can acquire one of these for a suicide run for forty or fifty million."

"How did you pay for one?"

"I got one for capturing you and Blackie. She's now made Russia a super power again."

"Everybody is going to know a Russian Mafia space shuttle took out the Bridge. That is not terrorism; it's suicide for The Russian Mafia, Inc. nation."

"You can't compare a corporatist nation's martyrdom with blowing up the Golden Gate Bridge, JANE."

"JANE is my dead sister you faggot. At the end of this countdown I win the game if I haven't forgotten that fact."

"Why don't you give in JUSTINA? Can't you see I have won the game? The Russian mafia is going to help me blow the Golden Gate Bridge with you strapped in next to me. What better orgasm could there be?"

"I'm frightened! Why am I tied down? I feel squishy inside. Did somebody rape me? Am I going to be gang banged again? First the Indians, then God and his spider Spot and now the Russian mafia. Thank God you're a faggot ANGELO. I don't think I have another fuck left in me."

"Don't make me laugh. Is that the way you win your games? By claiming you don't like to be raped by cross-dressing males? This game is not about rape. It's about free will. The will to win at the price of your life."

"Let me go then. I want to retire from terrorism. I'm sick of it all. GOD'S and yours and other self deluded nuts."

"Trust me. I know what I'm doing."

"Don't make me laugh? You look like an honest man, but you teach that promises are made to be broken. Is that what you call grounds for trust?"

"It is how you help fools become the fittest to survive."

"You say infidelity should be a man's creed?"

"That idea prevents innovative ideas from becoming obsolete."

"You are an amoral Maoist capitalist swindler."

"You think you know what morality is? You haven't even figured out what the red lips mean yet. They mean you're crazy, mad as a mud wart. Do you hear! As loony as a fucking leprechaun. And why? It's all because you are a compulsive-obsessive moralist, a nymphomoralmaniac. This is a choice that can land you in the nuthouse."

"You're right. I concede you're right. Will you make love to me now or can I take a bath first. I haven't had one in two years."

"It's important to remind you that I never sexually cauterize a victim until their festering wounds are clean."

JUSTINA attempts a sexy lap dancer mind fuck of ANGELO. "I want to wrap around you wearing a user friendly C4 backpack."

"A little bath in your urgency will never demobilize my denizens."

"I want to take my clothes off and make love to the whole world.'

"Your immorality is your immortality."

"If God knows the number of hairs on my head, you should be an angel and count my pubic blossom."

"Chairman Mao once said, "A true revolutionary is one who is willing to integrate himself with the workers and peasants".

"Give me some opiated head."

ANGELO takes out a pipe and begins to smoke.

" Who do you think I am?"

"You're my Princess Albert who lives in a can. How about coming up and smoking me some time?"

"You want to play with me? I'm a psychiatric artist who does computer models of what the world is going to look like after the explosion of the apocalypse bomb."

"My name is Empress Soon Will Sin. All I've had to eat this week is almond flavored duck. I'm so lame, I can hardly cluck."

ANGELO becomes the conventional psychiatrist again, "When did you have your first sexual experience?"

"When I was sex years old."

"What was the nature of that experience?"

"A boy made me kiss his penis."

"What did you dream about this week?"

"I dreamed I swallowed a huge slimy red whale and that he spouted and spouted until I thought I was going to explode."

"This dream clearly indicates a wish to bomb the National Aquarium."

"Been there done that. Come my dear. Integrate thyself with my prussic acid treated pussy. My red lips galore will make a woman of you yet."

"You offer me the crack of doom. You want to behead me JANE?"

"No way my dear. Freud is dead. Long live social diseases. Your problem Angi is you are not a normal psychoid. Otherwise you would recognize your Justi."

"Takes one to know one. Why don't you take a poll? Let the people decide the winner."

"Stop jerking off the people and let me fuck you."

"The time is almost up. You are a hopeless loser. I shall strongly recommend you be placed in an institute for the mentally unnecessary."

"No, please don't overwhelm me with your maggot monster mischief. I love you. Please let me fondle your dream machine and come on your compromises."

"Evolution is destroyed by lovesick fools who break the rules. I hate you JANE. Go back to your dirty hallucinations. You can never win at people's pool."

"Just once. Let your Justi. do it to you once and I will evaporate"

"No! And that is final."

"Sex is more infallible than an embalmed Pope."

"You are making it difficult for me to resist."

"Why can't you give me the only thing I really need?"

"You cannot be satisfied and you know it."

"No woman will ever be satisfied until men take their oppressive institutions and shove them up their collective asses. You don't care about satisfaction and you know it."

"There must be rules. There have always got to be prohibitions. Man must be protected from himself."

"You're doing your best to drive me crazy. You want me to kill myself?"

"I know what you want. You want to defecate on my determination."

"You wish. Your biggest fantasy is to preempt my pollution of grandeur."

"Only a spendthrift would call a psychiatrist a liar."

"Let me help you. I can make you whole."

"Have you ever made anyone whole?"

"It's my specialty."

"How long does it take?"

"Length is not a major consideration. It's more a matter of width."

"Don't you believe in principles?"

"I am a real woman. I deal in emotions. God spare me, I'm not a philosopher. I don't believe in principles. Do you?"

"I wear a chastity belt around my anal consciousness to keep them out of my black hole."

"I'm the mirror image of anal conscience, a celestial female in heat."

"Can you prove that JANE?"

"JANE? JANE who? I don't know any JANE anymore. I am JUSTINA, your fantasy dildo aren't I?"

"Good, then I win the game, because you have forgotten your real self named JANE. She was a mad woman who challenged me to this stupid game of amnesia."

"What have I lost? Am I going to be sorry or glad? How can I have lost if I don't remember what you've won?"

"I am sure you are going to be very happy you have lost, but I won't be able to collect on the bet until I can make you remember the game. Let's get this flight over with while I still have my sanity. Start her up."

JUSTINA pushes the button that causes the rocket plane to take off and it is seen to fly across the world to the Golden Gate Bridge with JUSTINA at the controls. Their navigation leaves a lot to be desired.

"We are coming in too low to crash it. Pull up JANE."

"Let's just fly under it. I'm too horny to die."

"Me too. O.K. Plan B. A statement."

"Maybe we'll be shot down by that star wars satellite defense fraud whatever."

"Don't worry. It's not working yet. It won't work for another ten years or more and by that time the corporations will have bought what's left of America and turned Star Wars into an interactive Internet game."

"That's not a bad idea is it? Will it be free?"

"It'll be free like the genome map, privacy, drugs, music, genetically altered food, use of public property and other things they have grabbed and used to up the bottom line. Now they are trying to trademark words."

"I thought they were worried about rogue states. But what happens if they find out who we are?"

"D.C. has been hit five times with suitcase nukes and nobody knows who did it."

"This is some ride. Are you sure this shuttle will fit under the Golden Gate Bridge?"

" No doubt about it. I made the calculations myself. Here it comes. Straighten her out."

They fly right into the bridge and everything goes down.

Chapter 26.

Virtual Resurrection

ANGELO'S face segues from a look of ecstasy at the moment of the crash to that of a red lip monster. There is a terrifying laugh; a scream and JUSTINA'S worst fears come true. He angrily smashes the consoles on which they have been playing their virtual sex game because he is a bad loser. This has been a game inside a game with a side bet. He opens a drawer, takes out a strap on dildo, and hands it to JANE.

JUSTINA-JANE taking dildo, "What is this for?"

"You won the game JANE."

"Oh, that game... Yes I am JUSTINA. You lose."

She begins to strap on the dildo.

"What am I supposed to do now? This thing's pretty big."

"The winner screws the loser. You can't back out now."

JUSTINA is hesitant. This is not the kind of 'screw' the loser she exactly had in mind.

"What a hard loser you are. O.K. You asked for it buddy. Get those pants down and lean over the bed. You're about to get revolutionized right up your faggot wormhole."

JUSTINA inserts the well-greased dildo into ANGELO'S anus and fucks him for all he can take. He screams with pleasure until she stops and rolls him over. He begs her not to stop. She then fucks him again in the missionary position. They finally collapse next to each other and fall asleep exhausted. The next morning ANGELO wakes up first and makes a call to a hospital for an ambulance to come to the house. JUSTINA is dragged into the ambulance in a straight jacket. She is laughing hysterically and insanely. ANGELO is standing by now dressed conservatively in an expensive Armani suit. He appears to be a normal professional male in every way. He is sadly shaking his head.

Chapter 27.
Angelo is a Hard Loser.

ANGELO ruminates on the unfolding events, "Why did she have to come to this? Just because she won a no nonsense game? Life is not a game. I did everything I could to cure her of her delusions of gender equality. You cannot save the world by bimbat terrorism. She tried to blow me up with that potato masher, but I was too smart for her. Only God knows what her problem is. I can only help those who are willing to compromise with what life is all about. Ah well. I should get the MacArthur genius prize for figuring out how to cure her violent temper. I deserve it. I'm drained to the core of my being. As for her! The latest prefrontal laser lobotomy will snap her back to normality and she'll soon forget these mad obsessions. This galloping figmentosa is a new disease likely to become an epidemic. Fortunately I've discovered the cure just in time. I'll probably get a medical Nobel Prize for its discovery. Although, it might be better to keep it a secret until I've done a double blind study to be sure I'm right. We cannot have big-mouthed misfits running around in the twenty-first century scaring everybody.

FINI ☐